ADDICTED TO MY THUG 3

A NOVEL BY
MISS JENESEQUA
AND
ARI

D1362367

Remember....

You haven't read 'til you've read #Royalty

Check us out at

www.royaltypublishinghouse.com

Royalty drops #dopebooks

Books By Ari:

- I'll Ride For My Thug 1 & 2 & 3

- Love, Betrayal & Dirty Money: A Hood Romance

- Young Love: Wrapped Up In A Thug

Books By Miss Jenesequa

- Lustful Desires: Secrets, Sex & Lies

- Sex Ain't Better Than Love 1 & 2

- Luvin' Your Man: Tales Of A Side Chick

- Down For My Baller 1 & 2

- Bad For My Thug 1 & 2 & 3

- Love Me Some You

- The Thug & The Kingpin's Daughter

~ *Note From Ari:*

Man we did it! Jenn writing this book with you has been so much fun! I'm so happy we decided to come together to make such an amazing series. To come together with all that we both have going on, this has been so rewarding. I look forward to creating more novels with you bestie as well as seeing what other works you have in store. Love ya hun!

To those of you who have read our series, thank you. We've worked very hard to create a story that each one of you can relate to. Not to mention every message, comment, email, and review has been extremely helpful. We truly appreciate the feedback and love you all.

To the top Diva of Royalty Publishing House, Porscha Sterling, thank you for your continued support! Thank you for always believing in us and pushing us to achieve our greatness. You are greatly appreciated and there is no other place I'd rather be then home with Royalty. It's because of you that all of this is possible & for that I am truly grateful!

Although our series has come to an end, there are still amazing novels in the works. Both Jen & I are working hard so be on the lookout! We promise not to disappoint. Enjoy!

~ Ari

~ *Note From Miss Jen:*

Wow... I can honestly say that I'm so happy and grateful Ari and I decided to write this collab together. I just knew that deciding to write with my royalty bestie was going to be easy, breezy and filled with nothing but fun! Love you, girl.

I've had a blast writing with Ari and I know for certain we need to do it again sometime. We hope that you enjoyed reading about Marquise and Naomi's relationship as much as we enjoyed writing it.

Thank you for all the messages and compliments on our book, it truly has been appreciated. The support has been amazing and I just thank God for having such patient, kind and dedicated readers like you all.

Even though this is the end of Ari & I's series, this isn't the end of us writing and still delivering amazing works out to you all. So stay alert for all our upcoming solo projects.

Shout out to our amazing publisher, the top queen herself, Ms. Porscha Sterling. Without her I never would have met Ari and never had the opportunity to work with her!

Again, thank you for all the love and support. Enjoy the story!

~ Miss Jenesequa xo

PROLOGUE

Knock! Knock! Knock!

"Yo! Baby, hurry your slow ass up, I gotta shower too."

All Naomi could do was laugh at Marquise's groans and complaints of her taking too long in the shower.

"The door's not locked, nigga. What's with all the knocking?"

Marquise frowned slightly before turning the silver bathroom doorknob and entering inside.

"I see someone's got an attitude this mornin'," Marquise noted, as he stood opposite where Naomi washed on the other side of the silver shower curtains.

"Attitude?" she queried in a confused tone.

"Yes, attitude," he repeated firmly. "Seems like someone wants to be taught a lesson today."

"Ooo... A lesson?" she teased him playfully. "And who exactly is gonna teach me that lesson?"

Marquise decided to keep silent as he pulled down his Ralph Lauren black boxers and took off his grey socks.

"Marquise?" Naomi playfully called his name, wondering why he had gone all silent on her for a minute.

It was only when she turned around to reach for her face wash that she felt a sudden cold air hit her back side and large, warm hands grip tightly onto her waist.

She gasped lightly once she felt his hands pull her back against his cold shower wall.

She was now forced to stare up at him as he stood in front of her, trapping her from trying to leave him.

"You were sayin'?"

"Marq... Let me go," she pleaded with a pout.

"Nah, you had so much to say before, why don't you go ahead and say it?"

Naomi couldn't think straight with her man being butt ass naked in front of her. All she wanted was to feel him inside her.

"Marq..."

"You don't wanna say it?" he queried with an arched brow as a smirk formed on his sexy, thick lips. "You was doing all that tal—"

Naomi instantly cut his words off with a quick kiss that rapidly began to grow more heated and heated by the second.

They had a few minutes to spare before they got ready to leave. Marquise was going to take her over to her old home this morning.

Naomi figured that Ty was on his way to work right now, so this would be the perfect time and opportunity to get some clothes and dip out, without him having to see her and her having to see him.

Two hours later, Naomi was on the passenger side of Marquise's Bentley, while he drove her to her old house to get the remainder of her things. She had a few things she wanted to take on her baecation to Dubai with Marquise, and she would rather get them sooner than later.

It was when he began to park nearby that Naomi realized that he thought that he was coming in with her.

"Baby, I'm cool on my own. I won't be long, it's just a quick in and out."

"Why can't I come in and help you though, bae?" he questioned her suspiciously.

"I promise, I'm cool. It's literally me just going in and out."

"You don't want me to come in or somethin'?"

"Daddy, no," she suddenly tried to convince him, seeing that he was getting slightly annoyed with her.

"I just don't wanna bother you and make a fuss. I promise that's it babe, don't be mad with me."

Naomi moved closer to him, pecking his lips lightly, and seeing how distant he was with her still, she moved to the side of his neck, gently kissing at his soft skin, knowing how much her neck kisses turned him on.

"Shit...Nao," he lightly groaned, making her grin with satisfaction.

"You still mad at me?"

"Ye... No," he whispered, still enjoying her kisses. How could he stay mad with his beautiful baby?

"I won't be long," she concluded before delivering one last kiss on his lips.

Then she left his car and walked to her front door. She brought out her key and unlocked the door.

It was weird that she was back here again, but she knew for sure that this was the last time that she would step foot into this house for a very long time.

She was totally done with Tyree.

Naomi gently closed the front door behind her and began walking towards the beige stairs leading to the second floor. It was only when she got midway up the stairs that she heard…

Noises.

Surprised that Ty was home, Naomi felt herself only becoming more determined to get up out of here, as fast as she could.

Once making it to the corridor leading to their bedroom, Naomi began to slowly stroll but suddenly stopped when she noticed various pieces of clothing on the floor leading to their bedroom.

Ty's jeans.

A skirt.

Boxers.

Bra.

His shirt.

A thong.

"Oh my… Ty!"

Naomi immediately felt her heart begin to race rapidly with fear and anticipation. What the fuck was she hearing right now? Moans? Groans?

And as the moans from the bedroom started getting louder, all she found herself doing was walking closer towards the ajar white door.

"You like that shit, huh, bitch? You want me to make you cum?"

"Yeah, nigga, make me cum right fuckin' now."

Naomi slowly pushed open the bedroom door only to feel her eyes beginning to swell up with tears as she looked on at the scene taking place on her marital bed.

Tyree was completely naked with his head deeply between Erin's legs as he gave her head.

She knew she recognized that voice.

"Oooo, right there," Erin moaned with her eyes tightly closed, one hand pushing Ty's head deeper and closer to her pussy, and the other hand fondling her left breast, playing with her nipple.

"Yaasss.... Yessssss, fuck, Ty," Erin loudly moaned as her climax began to come through. She started shaking and constantly moaning Ty's name.

All a frozen Naomi could do was look on with shock, disappointment, and confusion.

Was she dreaming right now?

Nah, she had to be, because there was no way that her husband was giving her "best friend" head right now.

"Turn around," Ty ordered firmly. "I want your ass up, face down while I'm fuckin' you this time."

This time?

All Naomi could do was stare at them both as they kissed each other passionately, as she realized that they had done this more than once.

Erin had been fucking Tyree.

Tyree had been fucking Erin.

All behind Naomi's back!

For how long?

Days? Weeks? MONTHS?

Once Ty broke away his lips from Erin's, she bit her lips sexily at him before beginning to turn around for him. That was until she spotted a figure standing close outside the door.

"N-Naomi?"

Naomi didn't bother staying after realizing that Erin had clocked her. Their eyes instantly locked and Naomi could see the growing fear in Erin's eyes.

"Naomi! Wait, Naomi!"

She simply turned around and began walking down the corridor to go downstairs. What was the point of staying and hearing what bullshit lies they both had to say? She had caught them both in the act and she wasn't about to stay to hear any details. She had seen more than enough.

I hope those muthafuckas are very happy together.

It wasn't until she heard Erin shout, "Naomi, wait... Girl, I did it for you! I only started fucking this nigga for you, bitch! So how the fuck you gonna be mad with me right now?" With that, Naomi stopped walking away.

Was she hearing correctly? Did this bitch just say she did it... for her?

Naomi no longer cared about wanting to leave. She felt like her whole body was on fire and was only getting angrier and angrier by the second, as she replayed Erin's words in her head.

She wasn't leaving until she beat a bitch's ass today. Severely.

Naomi quickly turned around, took off her silver hoops, and immediately stormed back inside the bedroom.

"Naomi, look, I can explain..." Naomi pushed past a guilty looking Tyree, ignoring his words before charging straight for Erin, who was now completely covered in Naomi's black silk robe.

Seeing the hoe confidently wear her clothing and freely have sex with her husband, on her marital bed, the bed she used to sleep on when they were together, had Naomi seeing nothing but red.

She charged straight for Erin, pulling her by her ponytail before pushing her straight to the ground.

"You're a dead bitch today, Erin Jones," Naomi spat before beginning her beat down.

The first punch sent Erin's head flying backwards.

Naomi didn't bother stopping though.

CHAPTER 1

"So he's giving you an ultimatum?" Erin queried curiously before taking a small sip of her water.

"Yeah," Naomi stated with a sigh. "He's giving me time to think about it but... the fact that he's even making me choose in the first place shows that he really wants to be in a deep relationship with me. Kids and everything."

"So, what's the problem? Ain't this what you wanted?"

Naomi nodded stiffly before speaking. "Yeah, it's what I wanted, but..."

"But what?" Erin questioned her through hooded eyes. "He loves you and he wants to spend the rest of his life with you. Isn't that clear enough?"

"I know this," Naomi stated. "But even after everything, I can't forget about Ty."

"What about him? Fuck that nigga," Erin retorted.

"Erin!" Naomi cried. "I can't forget about him, he's my husband. I'm legally married to him."

"But you don't want him anymore, girl," Erin reminded her with a smirk. "You want that sexy ass thug that blows your back out every time you enter his bed."

"I can't forget about Ty," Naomi repeated. "No matter how bad I want to spend the rest of my life with Marquise, Ty's still there."

"Yeah, he's still in the way, unfortunately," Erin responded with a frown. "What if he wasn't in the way though?"

"Then that would just be amazing," Naomi truthfully answered.

As her best friend, Erin knew she had to come through for her girl. It was her duty. And that's exactly what did she.

She got Ty out the way, so Naomi could go be drunk in love with her thug. It was the least she could do for her girl; all she wanted was for her to be happy.

Erin sighed as she looked down at her last text message from... Him.

Did you know?

She sighed deeply as she slowly typed back.

Know what?

Send.

That she didn't love me anymore.

Of course she knew. How could she not? Naomi was her best friend and told her everything, including the fact that she was madly in love with Marquise and was desperately trying to find a way out of her marriage with Ty. Now she had found that way out and Ty couldn't handle it.

Erin: *No I didn't know.*

Ty: *Are you sure?*

Erin: *Positive.*

Ty: *Okay, but did she ever talk to you about our marriage?*

Erin: *Sometimes she did.*

Ty: *Okay then. And when you sometimes talked about our marriage... What did she say?*

Erin: *That she loved you as the father of her children.*

Ty: *What else?*

Erin rolled her eyes with annoyance at the fact that this nigga was being so persistent toward this subject. He needed to let Naomi go. She no longer belonged to him.

Erin: *That's it.*

Ty: *Alright.*

Ty: *Can I see you today?*

Erin contemplated on his question for a moment before replying.

Erin: *Yeah.*

Ty: *Come round my house in an hour.*

Erin: *Your house?*

Ty: *She left me remember.*

Ty: *It's just me here.*

Erin: *Okay.*

Ty: *I could use some cheering up, baby.*

Erin: *I got you, Daddy.*

Ty: *You better.*

Erin sighed softly as she stared down at her bright phone screen.

Now that Naomi had finally left Ty, she didn't need to mess around with him anymore. She didn't need to pretend to like him anymore. She had messed around with him long enough for Naomi to slide her way out of his grasp and into Marquise's. That's all it was. A way of helping her best friend. But even as she said that she knew it was a lie.

Yes, at first it was all pretense, but now... she had developed feelings for Ty that wouldn't disappear. They weren't strong feelings, but they weren't weak feelings either.

An hour later and Erin was fixing her hair in her car front mirror as she took quick glances to the house across the road from where she had parked.

His house.

This would have to be the last time she let him touch her. This would have to be the last time she let him bend her over and this would definitely have to be the last time they fucked.

Once making it to the front door, she didn't even have to knock. Ty had already opened the door before she could even lift a hand to attempt to knock.

He quickly pulled her inside and shut the door behind her before pushing her against the cold door.

"Ty..." Erin felt her breathing hitch and a strong feeling of desire fire up within her as Ty began kissing on her neck. His hands found their way onto her waist and were now moving towards her ass cheeks.

"What?" he whispered in between his kisses.

"We can't do this anymore," Erin announced quietly, making Ty freeze in his movements. "She's my best friend."

Ty lifted his head from her neck and looked down at her curiously.

She felt nervous with him being so close to her, but she knew she needed to stand her ground.

"I've known her for years," she explained. "I can't fuck up our friendship over some dick. This is over, Ty."

Erin thought that after saying that to him, things between them would be finished and done with. She would be able to turn around, open his front door, and walk out without feeling anymore guilt for sleeping with him. She would just be able to get away from him and forget his existence.

Unfortunately, she thought wrong, because the second she tried to leave, Ty only pushed himself closer onto her and lifted her chin, so she was forced to look up into those mesmerizing honey brown eyes.

"You and her being best friends never stopped you from coming onto me, Erin," he stated boldly. "You remember that night, right? 'Cause I do. The night you called me over to your crib, got naked for me, and turned into my little freak for the night. Remember that night?"

Erin exhaled softly as explicit images of the things she did with him popped into her head. All the dirty positions, all the wet sheets, all the used condoms popped into her head, only starting to make her even more hornier than she was already.

"You rode this dick all night," he reminded her smoothly, "without a care in the world about your best friend."

"It was a mistake," she responded.

"A mistake that you kept running back to every night," he commented before gently pecking her lips. "I want you Erin and you want me..." His words trailed off as his hands made their way up her bare thighs. "There's no point in fightin' it."

Erin only kept still as she felt his hands begin to tug down on her panties and once he had pushed through, two fingers suddenly went inside her cave of wetness, making her moan.

"Uhh! Ty," she softly moaned as he pushed his fingers in and out of her.

"So fuckin' wet for me, baby," he seductively whispered, still sliding up and out of her, speeding up his motions. "I can't wait to get up in that pussy today."

All Erin could do was let him take control and make her feel good. There was no point in fighting what felt so good between them. It was better she let the magic happen now and the goodbyes happen later, because she wasn't playing when she said what they had going on was over.

Erin couldn't risk her best friend finding out that for the past couple of months, she had been fucking her husband.

CHAPTER 2

I got broads in Atlanta

Twisting dope, lean, and the Fanta

Credit cards and the scammers

Hitting off licks in the bando

What was taking her ass so long?

Marquise could only gently nod his head to the upbeat rhythm of the song currently playing on his radio, as he patiently waited for Naomi to come out.

Quick in and out she said.

Now here he was, getting worried about why a quick in and out was now taking longer than planned. He had offered to go in with her, but she had quickly deterred him away. Why did he even listen to her ass anyway? He was her man and if he said he wanted to do something for her, then he was doing it.

All Marquise could do was continue to worry and sit patiently, as he stared out the window to her house door across from him.

It was only a quick few seconds later when Marquise suddenly clocked an angry Naomi storming out her house. His heart began to rapidly beat with fear at the fact that she had tears coming down her eyes. What the fuck was going on?

Just as Marquise unlocked his car's door and began making his way out towards her, a beaten up Erin had now followed Naomi out in nothing but a black silk robe.

What the hell?

The more Marquise looked on, the more he continued to become confused, but once he stepped out and quickly approached Naomi, he immediately became solely focused on making sure his woman was okay.

"Baby, what's goin' on?" he questioned Naomi, pulling her into his arms and trying to wipe away her tears.

"Nothing, Marq," she quietly responded. "Just please take me home."

"Nah, Nao, something must be go—"

"Naomi, is that what the fuck you really gonna do?!" Erin shouted frantically, no longer trying to chase after Naomi. "You gonna beat me up after I just told you I did this shit for you?!"

Marquise watched as Naomi turned around to face Erin.

"Bitch, shut the fuck up before I beat your ass again," she threatened. "Stop tryna talk to me. You're dead to me, you stupid ass hoe. Some best friend you are! The best friend I ever had, trying to help me by sleeping with my husband all these months? You sick idiot!"

Damn, Marquise mused to himself. *She's been doing this behind Naomi's back for months?*

Just as Marquise began leading Naomi to his Bentley, Ty had suddenly made an appearance.

"Naomi, where the hell do you think you're going with this nigga?" he questioned rudely.

"Shut the hell u—"

Marquise gently cut her off, "Baby, chill, ignore his ass. Let's just go home like you wanted."

Marquise wasn't in the mood to start a scene right now. All he wanted was to take Naomi home, far away from here. She was officially done with Tyree, and Marquise would see to it that she never stepped one foot in this house ever again. And to know that he was sleeping around with Erin, the woman who claimed to be her best friend, was just foul. But fuck Erin. Marquise would be the only best friend Naomi would ever need from now on.

"Okay," Naomi replied quietly, feeling herself melt at how Marquise was trying to take control of the situation. She knew it was best if she just stopped acting crazy and let her man take her home.

"Naomi, where the fuck are you going with this nigga? So this the nigga you been fucking behind my back? I should have known there was something going on between you two that day at the mall!"

She entered into Marquise's passenger side seat, ignoring Ty's shouts and complaints from afar. She didn't want to hear anything he had to say anymore. Not now that she was done with him.

"Get out the car, Naomi! Get out right now!"

Marquise sighed deeply, trying his hardest to block Tyree out as he walked around to his driver's side, opened the door, and got in. But the minute he tried to shut his door, one word stopped him completely.

"I regret the day I ever married you, Naomi. You ain't nothing but a fucking stupid whore. I hope you had your fun with this nigga, because it's gonna cost you your kids now."

Whore.

Was Marquise dreaming? Nah, he had to be because there was no way that his baby had just been called the word whore. Naomi Evans a whore? The woman that he knew he wanted to spend the rest of his life with. The woman he saw in his dreams every single night and had been waking up next to for the past few days. Shit had to be a dream. Just a dream. No way had Tyree just called Marquise's woman that.

But it wasn't. And once Marquise realized that he had completely frozen in his movements of trying to get in his car and drive off, he knew exactly what was going down today. There was no doubt about it, someone was getting their ass whooped.

"Daddy, what's wrong? I thought you said we were... Marquise!" Naomi looked up with fright at the fact that Marquise had now exited his car.

"Stay in the car, Naomi," Marquise retorted before slamming his driver's door shut and making his way back round to where Erin and Ty stood watching.

"Why you over here, nigga? You wanna do something?" Ty questioned him, confidently taunting him.

Marquise only walked closer to him, his fists firmly clenching by his side. "You wanna say the dumb shit you said about my girl, to my face this time, pussy?"

"Yeah, sure, nigga. *Your* girl... who is really my wife... she ain't nothing but a who—"

Bam!

Naomi gasped as she watched Marquise deliver one hard hit to Ty's face. And even though the punch had sent him flying back, Marquise didn't stop.

Bam! Bam! Bam!

"Marquise, no!" Naomi cried, running out his car and trying to stop him.

Bam! Bam! Bam!

"Say it again, you bitch ass nigga! I dare you!" Marquise yelled, still delivering hard punches to his face and once Ty had fallen down to the ground, Marquise instantly began kicking into his stomach.

"So your ass can't speak now, huh? But you had so much to say just a few seconds ago," Marquise spat, still violently kicking Tyree.

One thing that Marquise couldn't stand for is people disrespecting what belonged to him. He never allowed it to happen, so why would he let it happen now?

"Marquise, stop! Please!" Naomi begged, pulling his arm and trying to drag him away. "Please Marq, he's not worth it!"

Marquise delivered one last kick to Ty's stomach, watching him groan and shake in pain before letting Naomi drag him away.

"Stay away from Naomi," he barked. "Or next time I swear I'ma put a bullet to your head. Real talk, nigga."

It was best he let her take him away, before he added a body to his already long list.

***

More tears began to leave Naomi's eyes once she realized what the two people she thought she knew so well had been doing behind her back for the past few months. How could they do this to her? How could Erin so freely and confidently decide to sleep with Tyree? How had she come to the conclusion that sleeping with Tyree would have been her way of helping her best friend?

She didn't need help from anyone but herself. What Erin had done was foul and Naomi knew she could never forgive her. Never ever. Who could forgive what Erin had done? And the fact that she had had the confidence to begin to fuck Tyree in her house without a care in the world, had Naomi in even more tears. Everything had come full circle and made perfect sense now. She felt so stupid.

Erin: *I'm sorry that you had to find out this way, but I'm not sorry for what I did.*

Erin: *I did it for you.*

Ty: *She seduced me.*

Ty: *Just come back home, Naomi, so we can sort this shit out properly.*

Ty: *You ain't leaving me for that nigga.*

Ty: *You see the shit he did to me today? He ain't nothing but a gangster!*

Erin: *You should be thanking me. I helped you get away from that nigga.*

Erin: *Without me, you wouldn't be happy right now!*

Ty: *I'm not letting you take my kids away from me. Try me, bitch.*

All Naomi could do was chuck her phone to the floor, wipe her tears away, and try her hardest to forget about all the shit she had been through today.

All the fucked up, backstabbing shit.

CHAPTER 3

"Baby, wake up," Marquise whispered sweetly to her. "You gotta eat something."

Naomi simply nodded her head 'no' and kept her eyes shut. She didn't want to eat anything. She didn't have an appetite at all.

"Bae, please... I know you upset, but you need to eat," he insisted. "I don't want you to starve now, do I?"

Naomi's eyes gently fluttered open as she looked up only to see Marquise sitting on the edge of the bed very close to her, so that he could place a hand on her back.

"Nao, c'mon," Marquise begged. "You've been sleeping all day, so I know your ass is hungry."

"I'm fine," she muttered.

Marquise shot a brow up at her suspiciously. "Naomi..."

"I don't want to leave the bed yet," she explained sadly.

"Alright, you want me to bring your food in here then? That's what you want?"

She nodded simply and before she knew it, he had left the room only to return with a silver tray in his hands.

"A'ight, sit up, sweetheart, so I can feed you," he instructed lovingly.

Naomi couldn't lie, Marquise's attempts to comfort her and cheer her up were slowly making her feel better. She appreciated the fact that she had him with her right now. He was so good to her.

Naomi smiled as she bit into the fresh strawberry he'd placed to her lips. It was sweet and after taking a bite, she realized how hungry she truly was. She continued to eat as he fed her random pieces of fruit. Although she was miserable on the inside, Marquise was doing everything in his power to make her feel better.

"I love you, Nao," he said while staring into her eyes.

She smiled. "I love you too, baby."

He handed her a glass of fresh orange juice and she began to drink. He continued to observe her as she glanced at him. To her,

Marquise was everything. He had truly been there for her during this hard time. He'd held her when she'd cried herself to sleep and hadn't left her side. Marquise truly loved her and proved that there was nothing in the world he wouldn't do to secure her happiness.

"Come here, baby," he said while breaking her train of thought. He set her plate of food on the night stand next to the bed, and slid next to her.

She did as she was told as she snuggled closer to him and placed her head on his chest. Marquise began running his long fingers through her hair while his other hand gently caressed her shoulder. Naomi exhaled, allowing the sense of comfort to overcome her.

"Nao, what you went through was fucked up. The shit was crazy as hell and fucked me up for a minute. I know that shit hurt you to yo' core. But I need you to know that we gone get through this shit together. I need you to know that everything is going to be okay," he confessed.

Naomi tried her best to compose herself. She could feel the tears beginning to well up in her eyes. She hated this feeling. The feeling of dread had her questioning her self-worth. She'd been betrayed in the worst way by two people that she'd never expected. Truth was she was devastated.

Marquise gently wiped away her tears and continued to console her.

"All I can think about are the kids. How do I tell them that they won't be seeing their auntie Erin? That their father and I can't even be in the same room anymore without fighting? There is no way in hell that we going back to that house, because, no matter how hard I try, what I saw will forever be embedded in my brain," she cried.

Marquise continued to listen as she confided in him. Truth was, he thought about the kids from the moment everything went down. He knew that Naomi would have to sit down and have a serious talk with the kids about the changes that were going to affect their lives. All he knew was he was going to be there every step of the way and vowed to make the transition as easy as possible.

"The questions that they are going to have. The ones that I won't be able to answer without crying or breaking down. I know I have to be strong, but it's easier said than done," she revealed.

Marquise gently placed his finger under her chin and lifted it until her eyes met his. Naomi stared at him with worried eyes and it made his heart clench. He hated to see her this way and it took everything in him not to put a bullet in both Tyree and Erin for what they did to his woman.

"We'll both sit down with the kids to explain everything. As far as their things, fuck all that shit, Nao. I'll get em' whatever they want and need. Ain't nothin' wrong with you crying, you human. You can't change what happened, but you have control of everything from this point on. The kids are going to be fine. Everything is going to be fine, okay?" Marquise declared.

Naomi nodded her head in agreement and closed her eyes. Marquise gently kissed her lips. She swooned under his touch. He slid his tongue inside of her mouth and she moaned as their tongues danced. He wrapped his arms around her and pulled her close.

"Marq!" she moaned as his hands explored her body.

He gently removed his t-shirt from her body which exposed that she wasn't wearing anything underneath. The site of her beautiful body caused his manhood to grow harder. He turned her body until she was lying on her back. Naomi bit down on her bottom lip as she watched him removed his clothes.

God he was so sexy. His body was nothing short of amazing. His chiseled chest and tight abs glistened in the light. His tattoos decorated his body and his manhood stood at full attention.

Marquise began kissing and licking her body, making soft circles around her nipple before sucking it into his mouth.

"Baby!" she cried while rubbing his back. He knew just what to do to make her forget about all the things going wrong in her life.

Marquise made his way down while tracing his tongue around her belly button. He kissed her inner thighs and Naomi held her breath, as she waited for the sensation she deeply craved. Marquise looked up at her with lust in his eyes as a smirk graced his lips. He knew exactly what she needed.

"Marquise!" she cried as he dove in. He gently sucked on her bud causing her back to arch. Her hands found his head and she threw her head back. God this man knew her like the back of his hand.

Marquise lapped at her middle and inserted his tongue inside of her. "Baby, you taste so fuckin' good," he exclaimed.

He had her turned on in the worst way. She needed this. She needed him to make the pain go away. She opened her legs wider as she felt herself coming closer to the edge. Marquise began to tongue kiss her pearl, causing her to scream out in passion.

"God damn!" she screamed as the overwhelming feeling over took her. Marquise grabbed her tighter as an orgasm rocked her body. All the while he sucked on her pearl, draining every drop of her sweet nectar.

Her body convulsed while she continued to writhe underneath him. She squeezed her eyes shut causing bright spots to cloud her eyes. She rode the wave of ecstasy and crashed when she felt it come to an end. This man—her man—had made her reach a peak that she'd never known was possible.

His hands caressed her body once again. Her body trembled underneath his touch. She opened her eyes only to stare into his. They were filled with undying and undeniable lust for her. He was ready as his hand moved up and down the shaft of his manhood. Naomi was dripping wet with need as she propped herself up on her elbows for a better view. She loved this man with everything she had and she planned to make him feel it with every inch of her body.

She attempted to move towards him, but he stopped her.

"No, baby. This is all about you. Let daddy take care of you," he cooed.

A smile graced her lips as his lips crashed unto hers. Her hands found his back and her lips moved to his neck as he inserted himself inside of her.

"Yes, daddy!" she cried as he filled her.

His lips found hers as their bodies moved in unison. In and out he gently moved. Naomi's nails dug into his back as he made love to her. Tears spilled from the side of her eyes. Marquise placed gentle kisses along her collarbone as moans escaped her mouth.

"Fuck, baby, you so wet for me," he moaned as he began to move faster and deeper.

Naomi's back arched and she wrapped her legs firmly around his waist. She was losing control of her body once again. Marquise gave her what her body craved. What she needed.

"Yes! Right there!" she screamed. He worked her middle like the pro he was. Naomi began moving as well, causing him to moan.

"I love you, Naomi. Fuck!" he yelled. They both felt the familiar sensation approaching as they began to pick up speed. Marquise pounded into her and Naomi made sure she matched his pace. Harder. Faster. They moved, as nothing but the sound of their skin slapping and moans filled the room.

"I'm cummin', daddy!" she screamed as another orgasm coursed through her.

"That's right, cum for daddy!" he yelled as he pounded into her, causing his orgasm to crash around the both of them while releasing inside of her.

Marquise lay on top of her as they both attempted to catch their breaths. He kissed her neck and the most beautiful smile emerged. Naomi basked in the afterglow of their lovemaking. They lay entangled in the sheets and in each other's arms. Naomi knew she was exactly where she was supposed to be. With her king. Her man. Her thug, and there was no other place she'd rather be.

Naomi looked towards Marquise who was staring at her as if she was the most beautiful woman in the world. She kissed his lips allowing their tongues to meet, before sucking on his bottom lip.

"You keep kissing me like that you gone be in trouble, girl," he threatened.

Naomi giggled. "Maybe I wanna be in trouble, Mr. Lewis," she countered.

Naomi bit her bottom lip as she felt his manhood coming to life as it rested on her thigh. She looked down before glancing back up at Marquise, who wore the sexiest smirk she'd ever laid eyes on.

"Trouble it is then," he said before pulling her on top of him.

CHAPTER 4

Naomi wrapped the towel around her body as she stepped out of the shower. She smiled as she wiped off her aching body. She was sore after their last session, but it was well worth it. She grabbed the lotion from the nightstand and began to apply it to her entire body. She looked up to find Marquise standing in the doorway watching her. He began to walk towards her with a look in his eyes that she was all too familiar with.

"Nope, don't even think about it," she warned as she began to slip into her lace thong.

"Think about what?" he laughed while wrapping his arms around her.

"Stop, Marquise, I'm not playing with you," she giggled, as he nuzzled her neck.

He picked her up and threw her on the bed before climbing on top of her.

"You saying no, but my pussy sayin' somethin' different," he smirked.

Naomi moaned as she felt his manhood between her legs. He was so hard and for the life of her she didn't understand how. They'd had sex so many times within the past twenty-four hours that she was sure he would be exhausted.

Even with that being said, she felt her middle get wet at the thought of him being inside of her.

"You tellin' me no? You know she speaks to daddy," Marquise declared.

Just as she was about to speak, her phone rang, causing them both to glance towards the nightstand.

"Don't even think about it, Nao," he demanded.

"Bae, I gotta see who it is. It could be the camp calling about the kids," she offered.

He rolled his eyes and climbed off of her at her response. The kids were the only reason he would ever agree. Naomi smiled at her victory as she slid to the end of the bed and grabbed her phone. Her smile faded at the sight of her mother's number on her caller I.D. She wasn't ready to talk about anything with her and had been avoiding her phone calls.

"You gotta talk to her sooner or later, ma. Just talk to her, Nao," he said before kissing her on the cheek and exiting the room. She watched as he closed the bedroom door behind him.

Naomi sat in silence as her phone began to ring again. She bit her bottom lip before answering.

"Hey, Mama."

"Well, hello to you too, Naomi. I was starting to think that you were dodging my calls," she confirmed.

Naomi bowed her head in embarrassment. No matter how old she got, the thought of her parents ever being disappointed in her still did something to her.

"Of course not, Mama. Just been a lot going on, that's all," she lied.

"Uh huh. Well I think it's time we have a conversation, don't you think?" she stated.

"Yes, ma'am," Naomi conceded.

"Today, Naomi," her mother ordered.

"Okay, Mama," she replied.

"Bring your little friend too," she demanded.

Naomi paused for a moment. Had she just said what she thought she said?

"Mar— Why Mama? I thought we needed to talk?" she questioned.

"No excuses, Naomi! If you're dealing with this man, then I need to look him right in the eyes. You hear me?" she demanded once again.

Naomi clinched the bridge of her nose with her fingertips before saying, "Okay, Mama. See you in a few."

Her mother hung up and Naomi ran her fingers through her hair. She felt an overwhelming sense of dread overcome her. With everything she had going on, complicating her relationship with her parents was the last thing she wanted to do.

"Marquise!" she yelled.

Marquise sauntered into the room and stood directly in front of her.

"Wassup?" he questioned with a worried expression.

Naomi stared at him for a moment. "That was my mother. They want to talk to me about everything that's happened," she declared.

Marquise took a seat beside her on the bed and grabbed her hand. He held it inside of his and said, "Are you ready for that? I mean, just because they want to talk to you doesn't mean you have to right now, Nao."

She smiled at his response. No matter what, he had her back, and she appreciated that. "I know, baby. They're my parents and they have every right to be worried about me," she stated.

Marquise nodded his head in agreement. "I understand," he responded.

"They want you to come, too," she replied while carefully watching his facial expression.

"For what?" he asked as he stood up and glared at her.

"My mother knows that I'm with you and I'm sure Tyree has called her to tell lies. Marquise, she knows you're important to me in order for me to risk everything to be with you. She just wants to lay eyes on the man that I plan to be with," she declared as she rubbed his shoulder.

"I don't know, Naomi. You gotta know that your parents might blame me for the part I played in all of this, ma. You don't know what type of shit that nigga been feeding them," he responded.

Naomi thought about what he was saying and realized he was right. But if he didn't go, then her parents would never get to know the beautiful person he was. She was positive that when they met him, they'd love him just as much as she did.

"Baby, we can deal with that when it comes. I love you and that's all that matters, alright? I got your back just like you got mine, and there is nothing that anyone can do to change that," she said while staring into his eyes.

Marquise remained silent for a moment while searching her eyes for any doubt between the words that had just escaped her mouth.

Once he was satisfied, he agreed. "Okay, baby. I'll go, but if it turns into some bullshit we leaving," he warned.

Naomi smiled as she stepped towards him and stood on her tippy toes before kissing him sweetly. They embraced in a hug and Naomi closed her eyes. She knew this was going to be an uphill battle, but as long as they remained untied, nothing else mattered.

"Let me get dressed so we can go," she sighed.

Marquise smacked her on the ass and replied, "Yeah, hurry up before I give yo' ass some more of this work!"

***

Naomi sat in the passenger side of his Bentley as they pulled up in front of her parents' house. That uneasy feeling had returned to the pit of her stomach and she was positive that Marquise could feel it too.

Just when she felt as if she were about to hyperventilate, she felt Marquise take her hand into his. She turned towards him and the look in his eyes brought a sense of calm over her. He nodded his head as a sign that everything was going to be alright. Naomi opened her door and Marquise did the same. He met her on the passenger side of the car and held her hand, as they both made their way to the front door of her childhood home.

"Y'all niggas was livin' like the Huxtables, huh?" he laughed. Naomi gently tapped him on the arm. She couldn't help but laugh and shake her head as he tried to lighten the mood.

Just as she was about to ring the doorbell, her mother opened the front door causing her smile to fade. Naomi watched as her mother stared at Marquise as she observed him from head to toe.

"Mama, this is Marquise. Marquise, this is my mother," Naomi awkwardly introduced the two of them.

"Nice to meet you, ma'am," Marquise said as he looked her mother directly in the eyes while extending his hand.

Naomi watched the encounter while holding her breath the entire time.

Slowly but surely, a smiled graced her face as she stepped forward and bypassed his hand. She embraced him in a hug which completely took Naomi by surprise.

Naomi finally released the breath she'd been holding and looked up at Marquise who towered over the two of them. He winked at her and Naomi felt as if her heart melted.

"Both of you come on inside now. I was just about to make lunch," she demanded.

Marquise stepped back and allowed her to enter the house first. He followed closely behind her and closed the door behind him. Naomi's mother had made her way into the kitchen and Marquise began looking at all of the photos of Naomi that lined the walls.

Marquise began to chuckle, as he observed what seemed to be photos of Naomi at every age as a child decorating the entire house. He stopped at a photo of Naomi with her two front teeth missing that caused him to laugh a deep throaty laugh. Her mother peeked her head out of the kitchen and smiled at the sight of them.

"Don't be laughing at my baby now, Marquise. She was adorable with her ponytails and snaggle teeth," she chuckled.

"Yes, ma'am, she was," he declared, while still laughing.

Naomi punched him in the arm while laughing as well. She'd never been embarrassed about that photo before, but somehow Marquise had changed that. He theatrically placed his hands up as if he were surrendering.

Naomi shook her head as she too chuckled. They continued to look at photos until they reached the ones of her children. She smiled as Marquise reminded her of how much her daughter resembled her. Her kids were beautiful and the sight of them made her heart yearn to be near them.

"You guys want some fresh lemonade?" her mother inquired from the kitchen.

"Yes, ma'am," Marquise responded as they both began to walk towards the kitchen.

They took a seat inside of the kitchen and sat across from her mother, as she stirred something inside off a pot on the stove.

"Um, Mama, what smells so good?" Naomi inquired as she allowed the smells to tickle her senses.

"Pot roast, mashed potatoes, and carrots, baby. I already made your favorite chocolate cake yesterday," her mother declared.

"Wait, yesterday? Why you do that when you didn't know that I was coming over until today?" Naomi laughed.

"A mother knows," she winked at her, before turning back to the stove.

Marquise smiled at their interaction as they continued to make small talk. Things were going smoothly and much better than she'd expected. Her mother seemed to be cool with the idea of her being with Marquise, which made her happy. After all, that's just how her mother was. As long as her daughter was happy, at the end of the day, that's all that mattered as far as she was concerned.

Naomi's mother was confident in the fact that both her and her father had raised her right. She knew that she would always put her kids first as they'd done for her. For that, her mother was grateful.

"So, Marquise, where are you from?" her mother asked.

Marquise cleared his throat before shifting in his chair. Naomi could understand why the question made him feel uncomfortable. She was aware of his troubled upbringing. Naomi held his hand underneath the table for reassurance.

"I grew up in Old National," he declared.

Her mother looked up from what she'd been doing and replied, "That's a really dangerous area in Atlanta, I hear."

"Yes, it is. It's on the south side and very dangerous," he declared.

"Hmm. So did you grow up with both of your parents? Any siblings?" she fired question after question.

"Mama?" Naomi interrupted. She was so mad at her mother for prying. She was being so nosey.

"It's alright, Naomi," he stated before gently squeezing her hand.

"I was raised by my big brother. He was murdered when I was a kid," he admitted.

This caught her mother's attention as she turned around to face him. Her eyes were full of sympathy. "I'm sorry to hear that, sweetie."

Marquise offered a small smile. "It's okay. It was a long time ago."

Her mother smiled and continued to fire questions at Marquise in an attempt to get to know the young man that her daughter was so smitten with.

"Do you have children, Marquise? What do you do for a living?" she asked.

Naomi glanced at Marquise, who was taking it like a champ. She was dreading her last question and cringed inwardly as he prepared to answer.

She mouthed the words "*I love you*" which made him smile from ear to ear.

"No, ma'am, no children yet. I own my own club as well as a few other properties in downtown Atlanta," he announced.

"Well, it seems you're doing very well for yourself considering all that you've been through. Your mother must be very proud of you," her mother conceded as she smiled at him before patting him on his hand. Naomi felt a sense of pride swell inside of her at her mother's words. Yes, her man had done well for himself and even though he was still knee deep in the streets, he'd made it, and that's all that mattered.

"A little too well if you ask me," a voice bellowed from behind them. Naomi froze at her father's words.

Fuck! And the bullshit begins...

CHAPTER 5

"Dad, glad you're finally home," Naomi said as both she and Marquise stood.

Her mother moved from around the counter and stood next to her husband. Naomi continued to stand next to Marquise with her hand neatly tucked inside of his.

"Imagine my surprise when I come home to find a Bentley parked in front of my home and *him* here in my house," he declared.

Naomi flinched at his choice of words. The way he was addressing him made her feel uncomfortable.

"Hunny, his name is Marquise," her mother confirmed in attempt to ease the tension in the room.

"Nice to meet you, sir," Marquise offered, as he extended his hand.

The glare her father gave could have frozen hell over. Not once did he even try to reciprocate the same respect that Marquise was offering him. In Naomi's opinion, he didn't deserve the slightest bit considering how he was behaving. Marquise lowered his hand and transfixed his gaze so that he could look her father in the eyes.

"Dad, what exactly is the problem? Mommy asked us to come here so that we could talk, but I see you wanted me to come for an entirely different reason!" Naomi boldly announced.

"The problem is you bring this thug into my home like everything is okay! The truth is he is the reason why your family has turned to shit!" her father announced.

Naomi felt heat rising from deep inside her. Of course he'd been talking with Tyree. His golden son-in-law who was the man that she was supposed to spend the rest her life with. How dare he take that nigga's side without listening to his own child first?!

"Hey, stop this mess! Let's all just have a seat and talk about things like adults," her mother offered.

Naomi felt Marquise's grip get tighter on her hand. She looked up to see him flex his jaw in an attempt to bite his tongue. It was because of her that he was keeping his cool, but honestly, she didn't know how long he could keep his composure and she didn't blame him. Her father was out of line.

"I will not sit down with him still here! How can you even entertain this shit?" he scolded his wife.

"Lower your tone, and she is our daughter! Don't you forget that while you take Tyree's word; he is not innocent in all of this!" her mother defended.

"No, I want his ass out of my house!" her father yelled.

"Well, if he has to go then I'm leaving, too! You don't even know this man, yet you stand here and judge him? You should be ashamed of yourself, Dad!" Naomi yelled.

Her heart was beating a mile a minute. Never in her life had she yelled at her mother or father. But, right now, he was pushing her to the point of no return. Her mother held her father's arm and stood by, observing the interaction between the two of them.

Marquise shifted his footing, still never taking his eyes off of her father.

"I don't need to know him, Naomi, because I know men like him! You had a family, silly girl! You gave that up for a damn thug who is going to drag you down into the gutter right along with him. You'll end up so far down that neither of us will be able to get you out!" he yelled.

Is that what he really thought? That Marquise was a low life, drug dealing thug? Naomi released Marquise's hand and stepped forward to face her father. There was no way she was going to allow him to disrespect her man. Not today; not ever!

"Yes, Dad, I had a family! I was married to a man that was fucking my best friend for God knows how long behind my back, but I bet he didn't tell you that, now did he?" Naomi yelled, no longer caring how she spoke to her father.

Her mother stepped back while placing her hand on her chest. Her father now wore the same shocked expression. Of course, big, bad Tyree had made them feel sorry for him with his lies of betrayal. Her father had fell for the hook, line, and sinker, too.

"Oh my God, Naomi!" her mother cried as tears welled up in her eyes.

Naomi's vision clouded. She felt a gentle hand on her shoulder and without looking over, she knew it was Marquise's way of reassuring her that everything was going to be okay.

"That man that you hold on a pedestal is no longer a part of my life and as far as I'm concerned, he's dead to me! There is nothing that you or anyone else can do to change that!" she cried.

Her mother reached for hand, but Naomi pulled away out of anger, giving her a wary glance.

"This *thug* as you called him, has been there for me every step of the way. Been there for both me and your grandkids in ways that Tyree never has! He loves me not because he says it, but because I feel it in here," she declared as she pointed to her heart.

Marquise draped his arm around her shoulder and gently kissed her forehead. Tears fell from her eyes as she continued to speak.

"Marquise and I are together, Daddy, whether you like it or not. I love him and if you can't accept that, well then that's on you. But, either way I'm moving on with my life and honestly, I no longer give a damn what anyone thinks of me! My decisions are mine, just that. Take it or leave it!" Naomi yelled before turning to grab her purse and heading for the door.

Naomi's father stood in the same spot he'd been in with a hurt expression on his face. Her mother followed closely behind both Marquise and Naomi as they made their way to the door.

"Naomi, wait!" her mother begged. It was no use as Naomi made her way down the stairs and climbed inside.

However, Marquise did stop to speak with her mother for a moment out of respect.

"Marquise, please take care of my baby. Don't hurt her; she's so vulnerable right now," she admitted.

"I love her with everything I have. I promise to always stand by her," Marquise declared, before embracing her mother and gently kissing her cheek.

He walked down the stairs and climbed inside his Bentley. He grabbed Naomi and held her as she cried into his chest. He rubbed her back as sobs tore through her. Marquise would always love and respect Naomi for standing up for him the way she had. A lesser woman would have handled things differently, but not his.

"Look at me, Nao," he ordered.

Naomi opened her eyes. "Fuck this shit, a'ight? Let's bury this and leave all the bullshit behind after today. Your dad just wants the best for you. He'll come around, I promise, but for now we gotta get shit in order before the kids come home," he declared.

She sat back in the passenger seat as he pulled away from the house. What used to be her safe haven from all of the curve balls had turned into something ugly and she just didn't know how to deal with that.

"I don't need to know him, Naomi, because I know men like him! You had a family, silly girl! You gave that up for a damn thug who is going to drag you down into the gutter right along with him. You'll end up so far down that neither of us will be able to get you out!" he yelled.

Her father's words echoed in her head as they rode in silence. Even though she loved Marquise and he loved her too, would that be enough? Would his lifestyle eventually become a burden between the two of them? Would the family life prove to be too much for him?

Naomi was filled with worry and the stress of it all was weighing so heavy in her chest. She looked over at Marquise who was driving while still holding her hand in his. He was a good man. He'd proven that to her time and time again. The fact was he even told her he'd leave that life alone if it came down to it, letting her know that he was in it for the long haul. For Naomi, that was enough and as far as she was concerned, she was willing to take this journey with her man despite the obstacles they faced.

Fuck anybody who was against them...

CHAPTER 6

Marquise wasn't surprised by Naomi's father's first impression of him. He wasn't surprised by the way that he had been treated by Naomi's father either, and frankly, he didn't care one bit.

Niggas didn't really like Marquise easily, and over the years Marquise learnt to deal with it because, honestly, he didn't really like niggas either. He wasn't a people person and he didn't like socializing and shit, unless he really had to for his business. He was all about his paper and his squad, anyone else could fuck right off.

Marquise just hoped that Naomi didn't let her father's bullshit ass words get to her. Yes, he was a thug. Violent, dangerous, and aggressive, but beneath it all, Naomi had been the only lady that had broken down Marquise's tough exterior and reached his true interior that was filled with nothing but love for her.

He didn't want her to take her father's words to heart. They didn't mean anything because Marquise was not going to ruin her life or kick her to the curb. She was going to be the mother of his children and be his wife one day. He was going to be the reason for her to go shopping for a white dress – *the only reason.* He was going to officially make her Mrs. Lewis.

All Marquise could do was lightly sigh as he planted a sweet kiss on Naomi's soft cheek and slowly crept away from her bedside. She was fast asleep right now and Marquise wished he could get in bed right next to her and sleep with her in his arms, but unfortunately that couldn't be done right now.

As Marquise began walking out his bedroom door, he took a peek at his diamond encrusted Rolex only to see the time, *11:30pm.*

Tonight, him and his boys had a serious job to do.

Blaze had finally worked out the meaning of Masika's dodgy text that she had sent randomly to Kareem's phone a few days ago. NDH stood for North Druid Hills and now the boys were setting out tonight to North Druid Hills, to find Anika and bring her back home.

Enough was enough. Blaze had suffered long enough without his girl and Marquise knew that if any mothafucka ever tried taking Naomi away from him, he wouldn't hesitate in tearing niggas apart. So he completely understood Blaze's determination to get his girl back, and he would be right by his boy's side, helping him.

***

"A'ight, so North Druid Hills is located on the outskirts of Atlanta," Marquise informed the boys as they stood over the round wooden desk, all hands on the large map of Georgia they were looking at.

"And if he's got them somewhere there, we gotta start looking at dope spots and warehouses," Kareem explained.

"From what I've found out, The Bulls had one main dope spot up there," Marquise said, pointing to North Druid Hills. "But no one's been movin' weight up there for a few weeks now. I even tried contactin' The Bulls' head. No one picked up."

"Well, the newest rumor is," Kareem spoke up, "Lyons took over the territory and robbed the dope spot."

"So basically, Leek owns the area now?" Blaze asked his boys curiously.

"Exactly," Kareem stated in agreement. "If he owns the area now, he controls what goes in and out."

"And he can control who he decides to keep up there or not."

"So we all thinkin' the same shit right now, right?" Blaze queried. "Leek's got Anika up there, right now."

Kareem and Marquise quickly nodded at their boy in agreement. They all felt and were thinking the same way. And they knew there was only one thing left to do right now. There was no backing down now and Marquise already knew this was going to be one long night.

"A'ight, let's go, niggas."

It was supposed to be a long drive up to North Druid Hills, but because of Blaze's ferocious driving, it turned out to be much faster than usual. Marquise knew for a fact that the only thing on Blaze's mind as he drove through the night, was reaching his woman. Nothing else mattered and nothing was going to matter until Anika was right back by Blaze's side.

Kareem and Marquise were especially glad that no cop cars had managed to follow them or tag them along the way. They were very lucky because if a cop car had pulled them over, they knew that Blaze would be in some serious trouble for the way he was driving. But fuck it. They understood his determination. He just wanted to get to Anika.

When finally arriving at North Druid Hills, Kareem pulled up the location of the dope spot that was originally owned by The Bulls and ten minutes later, Blaze pulled in near the warehouse.

They weren't sure what they were going to encounter when reaching the spot, but the boys were ready for anything. They were stocked up, each with their individual weapons, some hidden underneath their clothing and two guns in each of their hands.

Blaze held his red Russian AK-47 close by his side, while the other hand tightly gripped his silver .10mm. Marquise had his silver AK-74 in his left hand and his AK-12 in his other. Shit was about to get really messy up in here once the boys unleashed their ammo.

Slowly and slyly creeping round the sides of the warehouse, the boys decided to stay against the brick wall to run through their plan one more time.

"A'ight, so the buildin' has two entrances. The main one at the front, and the second one at the other side," Kareem explained quietly. "I'ma go through the back and try to break through if it's locked."

"And Blaze and I are goin' thru the fr—"

Blaze suddenly cut across Marquise, "Nah, go with 'Reem, Marq."

"What, why?" Kareem asked in a stern voice.

"I'm good on my own, I'on want you on yo' own though, 'Reem," Blaze responded seriously. "I'on want what happened to you, to happen ever again."

"It won't, nigga," Kareem fumed. "I'm a grown ass nigga, I can handle me."

"Look, I know that, 'Reem, but just follow my orders right now," Blaze said firmly. "I'd prefer it if Marq was by yo' side."

"And what if somethin' was to hap—"

"We ain't got time for the couples' counseling session right now, fools," Marquise quickly intervened. "We gotta get in and out, simple. I'll go with 'Reem. If niggas start shootin', niggas start shootin', and all we gotta do is shoot right back. We got this, just focus and stay on the job."

Kareem and Blaze nodded at Marquise with a determined facial expression, before separating to the locations they had assigned themselves to.

Kareem and Marquise slowly crept around the warehouse, keeping their eyes open and ears alert for anyone that suddenly crossed their path. Once they had finally made it to the back door of the warehouse, Kareem went to the opposite side and gave Marquise a signal, before they both decided to kick down the door.

Just the kicks from them alone was enough to bust the door wide open and just when Marquise noticed a shadow moving inside the pitch black warehouse, he started firing away. Kareem followed suit too.

Bang! Bang! Bang! Bang! Bang! Bang!

Once they were satisfied that the shadows were no longer moving, Kareem managed to find the main warehouse lights and quickly flick them on.

A long silver corridor was revealed to the boys. On the other end stood Blaze, completely surprised at the current turn of events as in front of Kareem and Marquise lay three men, now dead.

"Took care of these niggas already," Marquise loudly voiced. "No one else seems to be around. Leek and Jamal probably left for the night."

Marquise looked on as Blaze didn't continue to a waste a single second not searching for Anika. The warehouse was only one floor and along the silver corridor that he stood at the start of, he could see four separate rooms. Frantically, he began to search in each one and it wasn't until he got to the final room, when he noticed the steel locked door.

Even as he tried kicking down the door, it was no use. It wouldn't budge, no matter how hard he tried to kick through; the shit just wasn't going to come down that easily.

"Yo' B', I got an idea," Kareem revealed. "I saw a steel bar near the back, lemme get it and we gon' use that to break it down."

Blaze didn't bother replying, he just nodded stiffly at Kareem and focused his attention on the locked door keeping him away from Anika.

Marquise knew how frustrated Blaze was growing, especially with the fact that his bae was on the other side of the door. The only thing keeping Blaze away from Anika now was a door.

When Kareem finally arrived with the steel bar, Blaze immediately took it from him and aimed straight into the middle of the door. After two hard knocks, the door was finally hit down and Blaze didn't waste any time bursting through the room. Marquise and Kareem quickly followed him inside.

The room was a medium sized room with nothing but concrete flooring and brick walls. In the corner of the room, Masika sat. Her eyes widened with surprise and happiness, but Blaze didn't bother paying any proper attention to her.

"Ma... Malik?"

Blaze's head immediately snapped in the direction of the gentle voice that had suddenly sounded from the other corner of the room.

Marquise knew that now that Blaze had found his Queen, he would be good again.

~ The Next Day ~

Naomi sighed with happiness as Marquise lightly rubbed his nose against hers, before pecking her lips and then resting his head on her chest.

"Like I said before, bae... I'm so glad I have you in my life, just seeing Blaze's face when he saw Anika just made me appreciate the fact I have you in my life," Marquise announced sincerely. "And I don't want you to ever think that I won't be there for you. A'ight?"

"Yes, baby," Naomi replied. "I love you so much, too."

"You better," Marquise commented, lifting himself off Naomi's chest and looking up at her.

"I do," Naomi laughed.

"How much you love me?" Marquise questioned her with a childish smirk. "This much?" he asked, lifting up his hands and creating distance between them.

"More," Naomi stated with a grin.

"This much, ma?" He spread his hands out further.

"More," Naomi repeated with a chuckle. "Much more, baby. More than you could ever imagine."

Marquise's heart filled with joy, hearing Naomi tell him how much she loved him. He would never get tired of hearing her say it.

"You love me?" Naomi suddenly asked him curiously, making Marquise grin mischievously. He kept silent and just stared at her happily.

"Marq... Stop playing."

"You already know the answer though."

"I wanna hear you say it," she explained. "Do you love me?"

"You already know the answer, Nao," he reiterated, purposely trying to fuck with her now. "I don't really need to say it..."

Naomi couldn't help but roll her eyes with annoyance, and just as she attempted to get out of bed, she felt Marquise's arms suddenly grip onto her waist, stopping her from trying to leave him.

"And where yo' ass goin'?"

"I wanna grab something to eat," she coldly said.

"Oh, okay... I guess you'd rather leave then hear your man tell you how much he loves you," Marquise smoothly answered.

Naomi simply sighed with happiness and a small smile began to grow on her lips as she waited patiently for Marquise to tell her what she wanted to hear.

"I love you so much, girl, that I would die for you. Without you by my side I'm incomplete, sweetheart; you're my everything and I can't imagine my life without you."

Naomi continued to smile and once Marquise's lips locked onto hers, she felt amazing. He was everything and more.

He was her thug.

CHAPTER 7

Now that Anika was back safe in Blaze's arms, Marquise knew that things were definitely looking up for Blaze. He was no longer in a bad mood, just pleased and overjoyed he had his girl back. The only thing that had put a downer on their relationship was the fact that while Anika was in captivity, she had lost their baby. But Blaze didn't want them to dwell on the loss so much. He would rather them work on a new one.

Sadie and Kareem were also back together. Kareem had apologized for his stupid behavior at the hospital, and for not letting her know that he was married, but separated. However, they were good now and working on their relationship together.

Marquise was glad that his boys were doing well in their relationships, because he didn't want to be the only one completely in love and rubbing it in their faces all the time. It was good they all had their own wifeys.

Marquise looked down at his bright screen, carefully typing his message to his group chat with his boys.

Marquise: *No word on Leek or Jamal yet.*

Blaze: *Boys still searchin' right?*

Marquise: *Yup.*

"Baby, I wanna watch a movie," Naomi whispered in his ear while slowly running her fingers down the back of his neck.

"Uh huh, later, Nao, I'm busy..." His words trailed off as he kept his focus down on his phone.

Kareem: *It's been a week since we got Nika back. They gon' come lookin' soon.*

Marquise: *And we gon' get their asses.*

Kareem: *How Anika settling in B'?*

"Too busy for me, Marquise?" Naomi queried in a surprised tone.

Blaze: *She a'ight... Just been sleepin' mostly.*

Marquise: *In yo' arms I bet.*

Blaze: *Yeah, nigga, where else?*

Kareem: *A'ight, lover boy, so when you down for leavin' her home alone?*

"Naomi, just give me ten minutes, bae," he said simply, not bothering to look at her. "Then I'm all yours."

"I should have your undivided attention right now, Marq," she insisted, not liking how Marq seemed to prefer his phone much better than her.

Blaze: *I ain't sure… I ain't really thought 'bout it yet.*

Marquise: *You can't be scared forever B'.*

Blaze: *I know, I know… I ain't really that scared.*

"Marquise, are you even listening to me?" she asked. "Marquise!"

Kareem: *But you still scared.*

Marquise: *Just get some boys watchin' the house or somethin'. She'll be good.*

Blaze: *That don't sound like a bad idea. Yeah, I think I might do that, nigga.*

Marquise turned to face her with a calm expression. "Baby, I am listenin'. I'm just busy tryna talk to my boys right now."

And when Naomi gave him nothing but a rude look, he found himself drifting back to his vibrating phone. Was it his fault that his group chat was popping right now?

Kareem: *Do that. You gotta be okay with leavin' her by herself sometimes. There's no way those fools will try takin' her again. Especially not in yo' own home.*

Marquise: *I agree. Get some of the boys securing yo' crib and you straight.*

"Well, since you so clearly prefer your group chat more than me, I'ma watch a movie by myself." Naomi then got up and left Marquise on the couch by himself.

Blaze: *Yeah, I'ma do it. Thanks for the idea, niggas.*

Kareem: *You welcome.*

Marquise: *Talk to y'all later, Naomi trippin' right now.*

Marquise suddenly threw his phone to the side before getting up from his couch and following Naomi to his bedroom.

"Nao!" he called out to her. "I'm ready now."

"No," Naomi retorted, sitting on the edge of the bed, watching a shirtless Marquise enter the room with a frown. "You can go back to whatever you were doing before and leave me alone."

"Leave you alone?" he asked with a raised brow, sauntering closer to her. "Now you know damn well I can't leave you alone, Naomi."

"Well, you certainly can when you're on your ph— Mmh! Marq!"

Before Naomi could make out the rest of her words, Marquise had gotten close enough to pull her up and press his lips onto hers. Now he was kissing her hungrily, making her moan and heat up with a strong fire within her. How could she try arguing or stay mad at this man that she loved with all her heart? It wasn't possible.

Before she knew it, Marquise had lifted her thighs up and wrapped her legs around his muscular torso, still kissing her passionately as he led them out his bedroom.

Naomi didn't know where he was taking them and she didn't really care either, she was too lost in their kiss. Their tongues were only dancing and colliding effortlessly together in a battle filled with desire, lust, and love. And when he had finally reached his destination, he suddenly pulled their lips apart and set her on the cold kitchen countertop.

The second he started tugging at her black shorts, Naomi's excitement grew rapidly and she could only feel herself become wetter than she already was. Marquise always knew the right ways to spice things up in their relationship.

"We could make our own movie you know," Marquise commented, while pushing her shorts and thong down to her ankles and spreading her legs further apart.

Naomi only kept silent and nodded with a smirk, as she began helping Marq remove his sweats. She wanted nothing more than for him to be balls deep inside her right now. She was definitely no longer mad at him.

"You still mad at me, baby?" Marquise gently asked her as he wrapped her legs back around his torso, keeping them locked in place with his hands on her thighs.

"Maybe," Naomi taunted, wrapping her arms around his neck and pulling him closer to her. The more she looked down into his hazel eyes, the more she swore she was falling in love with him. Everything about him was so damn beautiful and she knew that she was one very lucky lady.

"You sure... You still mad?"

Naomi suddenly gasped the second she felt Marq's thick rod push past her tight walls. Every time they had sex, it took her a minute to get accustomed to his large size. You would think she would be used to it now with how many times they had sex daily, but she still wasn't.

"Uhh! Maybe," she moaned as he began to move in and out of her, doing it slowly to purposely fuck with her.

Every movement of his dick thrusting in and out of her, had Naomi rolling her eyes with pleasure and feeling over the moon.

"Are you sure you still mad?" His question was firm and direct, but it was still in a soft whisper that had Naomi losing her mind. Just hearing his deep, sexy voice in her ear as he continued to fuck her, had her on a high feeling of euphoria that just couldn't be described. She didn't want it to end either.

In. Out. He continued to move and used his large hands to rock Naomi up and down his dick.

"Answer me, girl," Marquise demanded before pressing his lips to her soft neck.

"Ugh! Marquise!" A sharp whimper left Naomi's lips as she felt his teeth suddenly bite into her neck. As much as it hurt, it felt good too, and she knew that the only reason she liked pain during sex was because of him. He had turned her into his little freak. "I'm not mad."

"You sure?" Marquise continued to push himself in and out of her, increasing his speed and going much harder than before.

The sounds of their skin slapping together, her moans, and his groans were the only sounds that could be heard in the kitchen, and Naomi could only feel herself getting closer and closer to her climax.

"I'm sure, daddy!"

"You love me? You love this dick?"

"I love you," she cried, just a few seconds away from cumming all over his heavenly pole that knew all the right ways to make her happy. "I love this dick!"

Marquise grinned happily hearing her moans, and he only continued to pound into her faster and harder, ready for her to cum.

"Cum for Daddy, baby," he ordered, sliding one of his hands off her thigh, to her ass cheeks and sticking a finger in her ass, just the way he knew she liked it.

Naomi felt her whole body begin to shake and her eyes tightly closed, as she felt that overwhelming feeling of her orgasm take over her.

Every single time they had sex, Marquise always knew the right ways to get her to that feeling of complete nirvana. She didn't understand how she had been living a life without him before. But she knew for sure that she was never going back.

***

Two days later, a meeting had been set up with the squad to discuss business, and apparently Kareem had fucked up his relationship with Sadie, again.

He had been caught fooling around with his old wife, Satin, in his apartment that he shared with Sadie.

"The bitch seduced me! And I was tryna explain that shit to Sadie, but she won't even listen to me. Every time I tried to speak, she threatened to kill me and she's crazy, so I ain't tryna risk dyin'."

"So you let her go?" Marquise queried with a silly smirk.

"After she strangled a nigga, of course I fuckin' let her go! I told y'all I ain't tryna risk dyin' yet. I gotta get her back first, man..."

"Well, you did fuck up," Blaze began in a firm tone. "After I told yo' dumb ass not to fuck up again, 'Reem."

Kareem sighed deeply before responding, "I know B', but it ain't my fault, I swear!"

"You let Satin into yo' crib, right?" Blaze questioned him through hooded eyes.

"Yeah bu—"

"And you let her kiss you first, right?"

"Yeah... But it wasn't m—"

"So how is this shit not yo' fault, fool?" Blaze asked rudely.

"It ain't! I swear I ain't even want her to come over, but how was I 'posed to get her to quickly sign the papers wit'out bailin' out on me. I had to make her feel comfortable and it worked, because before she tried that dumb shit wit' me, she signed the papers."

"Well, at least you got one good thing out of this whole situation, nigga," Marquise commented with a hearty chuckle.

"Yeah, I guess so," Kareem stated with a shrug. "Man, I just gotta get her back... She keeps on ignoring my calls, won't even reply to my texts, like what a nigga gotta do to get her to listen to me?"

"Stop fuckin' up," Blaze retorted. "Then she won't call things off between you two."

"Hey, like I said, it wasn't entirely my fault. I know I made some dumb mistakes lately with Satin, but I swear all that shit is out the window. She signed the papers, so now I gotta focus on Sadie."

"You do that," Blaze replied sternly. "Or else, the next time you fuck up, it won't be Sadie killin' yo' ass."

Kareem could understand why Blaze was so over protective when it came to Sadie. She was his cousin and even though they weren't cousins by blood, she still meant a lot to him. She was basically a sister to him, so seeing him pissed at her being upset wasn't a surprise.

"I promise, no more fuckin' up, I'ma make it up to her, B'. I promise."

"So what's the word on Jamal and Leek?" Blaze asked the boys curiously.

"They still ghostin'," Marquise informed him. "Jamal's stopped attending his court cases and he's neva out and about anymore. As for Leek, one of the boys spotted him."

"Where?"

"At the burned down warehouse, searchin' through the leftover burnt stuff," Kareem announced.

"Did he see where he went after that?"

"Nah." Kareem shook his head no before adding, "One minute he was there, then the next he was gone."

"They know we lookin' for them," Marquise stated with a frown.

"And they probably lookin' for us too," Blaze responded firmly. "The next time any of our boys spot any one of them on site, tell 'em to shoot them down."

"What?" Kareem queried with confusion. "I thought you wanted to deal with them both."

"I did," Blaze said with a deep sigh. "But I can't."

"But B', they took yo' girl. Surely you must want to deal with them both in the worst possible wa—"

He cut Marq off. "I did, Marq, I still do. But I made a promise to Anika not to kill Jamal. She clearly don't want me killin' nobody, so imagine how she'll feel knowin' I killed Leek, too. I just gotta learn to let this shit go and move on. I got Anika back, so what's the point?"

"The point is, they plotted against us all and tried to bring our empire down," Kareem snapped, banging his fist on the wooden table in front of him. "Fuck a promise, nigga! Those niggas need to pay."

Blaze shot Kareem a rude glare, seeing that he was getting hyped up over the whole situation.

"Look, I can't break my promise to Anika," Blaze explained. "I'm not like you, 'Reem. I don't keep fuckin' up and makin' my girl pissed." Kareem kept silent at his harsh words.

Marquise had actually been thinking about a way to deal with Jamal legally. The fact that Jamal, an attorney, had suddenly sparked up so much interest to help a rival dope gang of theirs, had Marquise thinking that Jamal was a very dodgy guy. He wasn't as normal as the community portrayed him out to be. There had to be deep, dark secrets he was hiding from everyone else. And Marquise wanted to know every last bit of them.

"Maybe you ain't even gotta break Nika's promise," Marquise suddenly voiced. "You still got that number for the attorney Jayceon gave you, B'?"

"Yeah, why?"

"I got an idea. I'm not sure if it'll work, but it should," Marquise declared contently. "If I'm right, you won't have to get yo' hands in any blood, Blaze."

"Or Marq and I could just kill both those motherfuckers for ya'," Kareem intervened confidently.

"Nah," Blaze quickly shut him down. "I like Marq's idea better. Tell me more, Marq."

Just as Marquise began to explain his sudden theory, one of the Knight Nation boys knocked on the door twice and stepped into the room.

"Yo, guys," he greeted them gently.

It was Tyrell, one of the niggas that Blaze had hired a few months back, because he seemed like a hard worker and down for earning some quick cash.

"Sup, Ty?" Marq greeted him friendly.

From the blank look now plastered on Tyrell's face, the boys knew that something was up.

"Me and a few of the others found somethin' near the back entrance."

"What was it?" Kareem asked.

"I think y'all should come take a look for yo'selves," Tyrell insisted.

So Blaze, Kareem, and Marquise got out their seats, made their way out of their main meeting room, and headed to the back entrance of their warehouse.

When they finally arrived, they all noticed the black body bag that had now been unzipped open, allowing the body to be seen.

Blaze instantly caught a glance of the face and he had to do a double take.

"What the fuck?"

Her head had been chopped off from the rest of her body, so in the body bag lay her headless body and her head just lying above. Everyone just looked ahead with shock, at the dead female lying in the body bag.

Masika Brooks. Blaze's ex-girlfriend and the girl that had managed to worm her way onto Marquise's dick.

"Shit, man," Marquise spoke up. "Those niggas so disrespectful dumpin' her here."

Leek and Jamal definitely had to pay for all the shit they had done. From taking Anika and now bring Masika's dead body to their door.

They had to be punished.

CHAPTER 8

"He said he was sorry, and he wants to apologize in person, Naomi. But he still doesn't agree with you seeing Marquise. He still believes he's nothing but a gangster and is no good for you."

Naomi sighed as she continued to listen to her mom speak.

"I don't agree with him, because I know how much Marquise means to you and how happy he makes you, sweetheart. I could see it in your eyes when you came round with him and just seeing the way you two were in love, I just knew he's the man for you."

"Thank you, Mom," Naomi stated calmly. "I know how hard it is putting up with Dad and hearing him try to force his opinions on you."

"Well, he can try all he likes, but I'm not gonna change my mind! I like Marquise and if he doesn't then he can carry on being a fool somewhere else."

"I'm not coming down there again for a while though, Mom. If you wanna see me then we can arrange to meet up somewhere, but I'm definitely not stepping foot in the house again."

"Why not, baby? That's a bit too much."

"I know, Mom, but I just can't. I'd rather stay away from that place for a while and just focus on the things that make me happy. Don't take it personal, I'll get over what Dad said soon."

"It's alright, huni, I understand," her mother replied. "Just understand that I'm a phone call away, and if you ever want to talk then I'm here for you."

"Thank you, Mom. I love you."

"I love you, too, Naomi. Take care of yourself, my grandkids, and your man."

Today, Naomi had a surprise for her baby.

She was going to go pick up the kids from summer camp today and bring them straight back home. Their new home with Marquise.

Naomi wasn't sure how she was going to explain to the kids about what was happening between their father and her, but she knew that Marquise would be right by her side, helping her explain. And that's one of the many reasons why she couldn't stop loving him. He was always there for her, no matter what.

Marquise had left the house very early in the morning to go meet up with his boys, so Naomi had woken up to an empty bedside unfortunately.

However, now she was getting ready to leave the house so that she could go get her babies that she had missed so much. It wasn't until she reached for her LV handbag on the dining table that her phone began to ring.

Remember all the nights we used to fall through

Wondering why you don't fall through

On the late late nights I used to call you

Wondering why I don't call you

And it's déjà vu

The seductive sounds of "TWENTY88" filled Naomi's ears and once finding her phone and seeing the caller I.D, she instantly frowned and sucked her teeth with annoyance. Why was this bitch calling her?

She had nothing to say to her and she certainly didn't want to hear anything she had to say to her. She was dead to her.

Once her phone had stopped ringing, a wave of relief passed over Naomi, but it was quickly short lived once a text message notification popped up on her screen.

Erin: *Pick up my call, Naomi!*

Erin: *You can't keep ignoring me.*

No... I can't keep ignoring you, Naomi mused. *But I can block your ass.*

Naomi decided to do just that, slightly irritated at the fact that she hadn't bothered doing it before. Once Erin's number had been blocked, Naomi chucked her phone back into her bag and set out on her journey of going to pick up her wonderful kids. She couldn't wait to see Chris and Josie Evans. They were the only two people, including Marquise Lewis, of course, who never failed to put a smile on her face. She loved them all so much.

It took her half an hour to arrive at the summer camp and after parking her car, Naomi left with a bright smile on her face because of the fact that she was about to see her kids after these two weeks. These two life changing weeks.

She just hoped that her kids were able to adjust and adapt to the new environment of living with Marquise.

Once arriving at the summer camp entrance, Naomi pushed through the glass building doors to head to the main front desk booth. She noticed the small queue of parents ahead who had also come to pick up their children, but it wasn't them who suddenly had her full of anger.

It was the man currently at the front of the queue trying to persuade the lady at the front desk that he was the father of two kids by the name of Christopher and Josie.

"I'm afraid I can't let you pick them up, sir, you weren't the one who signed the consent forms or dropped them off two weeks ago," the lady informed him seriously. "I can't let them go with you. Only their mother, Naomi Evans, has permission to take them home today."

Naomi couldn't believe what this guy was trying to do right now. Was he stupid or something?

"Well... Naomi Evans passed away last week unfo—"

"Tyree! What the hell do you think you're doing?" Naomi shouted, cutting his words off and walking closer to the front desk.

Naomi quickly sent a prayer up to the Lord above...

God, please don't make me have to kill this nigga in front of all these people, please God. We both know jail isn't for me. But if I have to kill him, then you know I will. I'll just have to get used to a new environment away from Marquise. Because this nigga has me all the way fucked up if he thinks that I'm going to stand here and take this disrespect.

Naomi wasn't about to back down. Not with her precious kids involved. Tyree had chosen the wrong day to mess with her.

CHAPTER 9

The look on Tyree's face was priceless. It was as if he'd seen a ghost walk into the building, but there wasn't one. It was Naomi in the flesh and she was prepared to give him the show of his life. She was taking the gloves off.

"I asked you a question, Tyree? Why are you here to get my kids?"

Guilt was written all over his face as he looked into her eyes. But Naomi didn't give a damn considering he'd just told the woman at the counter that she was dead.

"Let me tell you something, we can do this shit the easy way or the hard way. But, I'm only gonna give you one chance to decide. Now what's it going to be?" Naomi questioned as she stood in front of him with her hand firmly planted on her hip.

"What do you mean? Naomi, these are my kids, too, and if their daddy wants to see them I should be able to!" Tyree declared.

Who did this nigga think he was playing with? Was he thinking about his kids when he was sticking his dick inside of her best friend in the home they shared with the same children he was now so concerned about?

Naomi stepped closer to him so that there was barely any space. She stared him directly in the eyes as a scowl became permanently etched on her face.

"Don't play games with me, Tyree! You just told this woman that I was dead and your disrespectful ass thinks that you gonna be anywhere near my kids? You gotta be out yo' damn mind. Get the hell out of this building before I embarrass yo' ass!" she threatened.

The other parents couldn't help but watch the scene in front of them unfold. Everyone stood around in utter disbelief and shock at their behavior. Naomi was too angry to feel embarrassed right now. All she wanted to do was pick up her kids in peace, but no, Tyree just couldn't let her do that.

"Sir, I think that it's time for you to leave," the woman behind the counter declared in an attempt to diffuse the situation before it took a turn for the worst.

"Fuck that, I ain't going nowhere! You ain't taking my kids from me, Naomi," he announced.

Naomi chuckled. Did this nigga really think he had a choice in the matter?

"Leave Tyree," she countered.

"Look I know we going through some thin—" he attempted to speak.

"Are you dumb or deaf? Save that shit because God knows I couldn't care less about anything you have to say!" Naomi yelled as she folded her arms across her chest.

Tyree's chest heaved in frustration and anger. Who was this woman standing in front of him? What happened to the woman he married? The woman that would do anything and everything in her power to ensure her family was happy?

He couldn't believe that she was treating him this way. Finally understanding that she wasn't going to budge, he shot her a glare that would have sent chills through most women. Except Naomi didn't care and grinned at his response instead. This pushed him over the edge.

"You ain't shit, Naomi, with your triflin' ass! You call yourself a mother, but you ain't shit but an evil ass bit—" Tyree attempted to yell.

Slap!

Naomi's chest heaved after throwing her hand so hard into the side of his face. She was pissed and had every right to be. Tyree continued to disrespect her and she was sick of it. She was ready to whoop his ass and she didn't give a damn who saw her do it either.

A shocked Tyree stumbled back and placed a hand on the side of his face. He turned to look at Naomi with pure fire and hatred in his eyes.

"That's it, sir, I'm calling security! You need to leave now or else you will go to jail!" the woman from behind the desk yelled.

Out of the corner of her eye, Naomi notice the woman picking up the phone. She whispered something before quickly hanging up and stepping from around the counter. All the while, Naomi hadn't moved an inch. She was standing her ground and she dared this nigga to try her.

"All I want to do is see my kids!" Tyree countered.

"Absolutely not! My kids don't need to be around you or anyone else who would dare to disrespect their mother in such a way! What you need to do is get in the damn car and go before the police come," she threatened.

Tyree took a step towards her and Naomi dropped her bag on the floor next to her feet, prepared to tag his ass. Just as she was prepared to swing, security emerged through another set of glass doors where the children were currently being held.

"Sir, I suggest you think again! Don't you take another step or else we will have to taser you!" security yelled.

Naomi glanced at the woman that originally stood behind the counter, who was now standing a few feet from Naomi. A sense of relief washed over her face as security marched in to escort Tyree off of the property.

Naomi had to admit that she was relieved as well. Was she prepared to go blow for blow with Tyree? Hell yeah she was, but did she want to? Hell no. Not with her kid's mere feet away from her.

"Let's go, sir. Leave the premises now," security demanded, as four guards marched towards him.

A defeated Tyree raised his hands as a sign that he was giving up, all the while glaring at Naomi as if she were the lowest scum on the earth. He backpedaled towards the door, just as a guard placed a hand on his arm and Tyree snatched away.

"I know the way out! Keep yo' fuckin hands off of me!" Tyree yelled as he exited the building and climbed into his car. He sped off into the distance leaving nothing but an angry cloud of dust behind him.

Naomi closed her eyes and placed her fingers on the bridge of her nose. What had her life become?

"Ma'am, are you alright? Do you need us to call the police to escort you home?" the officer questioned.

Naomi opened her eyes to stare at him as she became all to painfully aware that all eyes were now on her. She glanced around at all of the individuals who stood idly by.

"No... I'm fine. I just want to get my kids and leave, if it's alright," she countered.

"Of course," he nodded his head before turning on his heels to get Josie and Christopher.

Naomi felt the tears stinging her eyes, but she refused to allow them to fall. She'd already cried so much, and frankly, she was tired of feeling weak. Most of all she was tired of the drama that her life had become so consumed with. All she wanted to do was get her babies and head home to her man.

Just as she began to replay the events that had taken place in her head, out came running both Josie and Christopher with the biggest smiles on their faces. Naomi smiled as well as they both ran into her arms. She held onto them while placing sweet kisses all over their faces. God knows she'd missed them so much and just being in their presence had changed her entire mood.

"Mommy, we missed you so much!" Josie cooed.

"Yea, Mama, we missed you!" Christopher added as they continued to hug each other.

"Mommy missed you both so much! I don't know how I made it through two whole weeks without you!" she countered.

"Mommy, are you going to squeeze us to death?" Josie questioned.

Naomi laughed at her daughter. She hadn't realized that she had been squeezing them so tight.

"Sorry, baby. Let's get out of here," Naomi countered as she picked her purse up from the floor and headed for the door.

She cautiously looked around for any sign that Tyree may have returned, and once she was sure that he was nowhere in sight, she headed for the car with her kids right on her heels. She hit the button on her alarm which popped her truck open so that they could load their suitcases inside. She closed the truck and walked to the driver's seat as both of the kids climbed inside the back seat.

"Buckle up," Naomi demanded.

She smiled as she observed her babies through the rear view mirror. They were so innocent in all of this. Their lives would be forever changed whether she liked it or not. How was she going to tell them that they wouldn't be going home to sleep in their own beds? Naomi sighed, started her car, and began to drive.

"Mommy, where is Daddy?" Christopher asked.

The moment she'd been dreading had arrived. Naomi took a deep breath...

Here goes nothing...

CHAPTER 10

Naomi sat in the living room at Marquise's house as the kids sat directly across from her on the couch. The devastated expressions on their faces broke her heart. She only wanted what was best for her kids and right now, all she felt was that she was causing them nothing but pain.

After Christopher asked about their father, Naomi told them that they'd talk about that when they reached their destination. She just refused to have this conversation with them while driving and not being able to look them directly in the eye. She made them something to eat while she gathered her thoughts and established the best way to approach the situation. Once they'd finished eat and cleaning up the kitchen, she sat them both down so that they could have their talk.

Now that they were sitting face to face, and their tear-filled eyes bore holes through her, all she wanted to do was crawl into herself. She wished she could make everything okay, but there was nothing she could possibly do at this point except tell them the truth.

"But, Mommy, I don't understand why we can't go home? Are we never going to see Daddy again?" Josie questioned as tears spilled from her eyes.

Naomi felt her heart clench. "Mommy and Daddy just don't need to be around each other right now, that's all. Of course you'll be able to see him. He just needs some time to himself."

"And this is Mr. Marquise's house? Does Daddy know where we are?" Josie countered.

"Yes, sweetie, this is his house. No, Daddy doesn't know that we're here, but he knows that you both are safe and sound."

"Is Mr. Marquise coming back here to stay with us?" Christopher asked.

"Yes he is, but right now he's at work. He'll be back soon."

"Did Daddy do something really bad, Mommy?" Christopher asked with worried eyes.

Naomi felt herself tearing up and tried her best to compose herself before answering her child.

"Baby, sometimes grownups fight and that's okay. Right now it's just best if daddy and I are apart. But, everything is going to be alright, I promise."

"Okay, Mommy," Josie chimed.

Naomi smiled as she watched her daughter. She was trying her best to put on a brave face even though her little mind was swirling with thoughts. Naomi stood up and stepped in front of her kids. She bent down and embraced the both of them, allowing them to cry on her shoulders.

She squeezed her eyes shut and allowed the tears she'd been holding in to fall. She cried for her failed marriage, the betrayal, and lies that had caused so much pain for them all. The looks on her babies' faces crushed her. How could she honestly answer any questions they had when in actuality she had no clue what would happen next? All her babies knew was that when they'd left for camp they'd had both parents, and now they only had one.

"I know you guys must be exhausted. It's kind of late, so I want you both to go and brush your teeth so that you can get ready for bed, okay?" Naomi declared.

Both Josie and Christopher nodded their heads in agreement before moving to retrieve their toothbrushes from their luggage that still sat by the front door. She silently watched the two of them as they walked down the hall to the bathroom.

Naomi turned her back and placed her hand over her mouth, as tears poured from her eyes. This by far had been the hardest thing she'd ever had to do. The heartache that her babies were experiencing right now was just so unreal.

She grabbed her phone and began to text Marquise while wiping the tears from her face.

Naomi: *Baby, when are you coming home? The kids are here.*

Marquise: *Wrappin' shit up now. How are they?*

Naomi: *Ok I guess...*

Marquise: *You guess?*

Naomi*: They're scared and worried. I told them as much as I could without telling them the whole truth.*

Marquise: *Without me?*

Naomi: *Sorry... they asked where he was. It couldn't wait.*

Marquise*: And you?*

Naomi exhaled as more tears streamed from her eyes.

Naomi: *I need you right now.*

Marquise: *Be there in 20 minutes.*

Naomi: *K.*

"Mommy, we're finished," Josie stated.

Naomi quickly wiped away her tears before turning to face her kids. They both stood at the entrance of the hallway with sorrow filled expressions.

"Let's get you two into bed," she said as she approached them and held out her hands. They each took a hand into theirs and walked beside their mother, as she led them to the bedrooms that they'd be sleeping in.

"Mommy, can we sleep together?" Christopher asked.

She smiled at her baby boy. For years they'd been separated and sleeping in their own bedrooms, but right now all he wanted was to be next to his sister.

"Of course you can, baby," she responded.

Naomi watched as they slid into bed next to each other. She turned off the light that sat on the nightstand beside the bed. She then tucked them in and kissed them both after they said their prayers as they did every night.

"Goodnight, kids," she said as she exited the room and slightly cracked the door.

Naomi walked down the hallway and stepped into the kitchen. She began to straighten things up around the house to keep herself busy. Anything to keep her mind from drifting back to that day. Anything to keep herself from feeling the pain. She sighed as she grabbed a wine glass and a bottle of her favorite wine from the fridge.

Naomi poured herself a glass and drank it down quickly, allowing the sweet substance to take effect. She poured herself another glass and gulped it down halfway before deciding to sip the rest. The wine was beginning to take effect and she welcomed it. She closed her eyes and continued drinking with the only goal being to get as inebriated as possible. Right now, all she wanted was to be held by her man.

***

Marquise sat on the edge of the bed, intently listening to what Naomi was saying. She wasn't crying anymore, but the pain in her voice was still there. The intensity of the words that she spoke cut him deep. He was trying his best to hold his composure, but right now all he wanted to do was put a bullet in Tyree's head. He had disrespected his woman one too many times and Marquise refused to let him get away with it.

"I just don't know what to do."

Marquise didn't speak. He allowed her to talk and to get it all out of her system. It was evident that she'd been drinking and crying before he got home.

"I hate Tyree! I just want him to leave me the hell alone so that I can move on with my life. He keeps texting me, begging to see the kids and I just can't do that right now," Naomi confessed.

Just as Marquise was about to respond, his phone began vibrating in his pocket. He ignored the ringing and continued to listen to Naomi while she vented. But, then his phone began to ring again. He took it out of his pants pocket and glanced at the screen with a confused look on his face. He scrunched up his eyebrows at the fact that an unknown number was calling him once again. Over the past few months, someone had been calling him and when he answered, they would remain silent. It was really starting to bother him because for the life of him, he couldn't figure out who it was. Even more so, after what Blaze had just went through with his girl, Anika, Marq was on high alert for any sign of bullshit.

"Marq, are you even listening to me?" Naomi questioned breaking his train of thought.

Marquise hit ignore on his iPhone before shoving it back in his pocket. The last thing he wanted Naomi to think was that he was ignoring her.

"Yes bae, I'm listening to everything you saying," he responded.

"It don't seem like it," she declared with a frown.

Marquise moved closer to her and looked her directly in the eye.

"Cut that shit out. You know I heard everything you said. Now it's my turn to talk and you need to listen."

Naomi looked him in the eyes and nodded her head in agreement. She valued Marquise's opinion and definitely wanted to hear what he had to say.

"Nao, you gotta stop stressin'. This shit is beyond your control and nothing will change that. You can replay what happened over and over in your head, but at the end of the day it is what it is. What you do from here on out is what makes the difference. Shit, if it was up to me, neither one of they asses wouldn't breathe another breath on this earth."

Naomi gave him a knowing look. "Marq, he's their father. Even though he ain't been much of a man to me, he has the right to see his kids."

Marquise narrowed his eyes as he looked at her. "Fuck that nigga and his rights! That's the problem right there! Nigga think he got the right to disrespect you too, huh? You know how I am, Nao, so don't try that shit with me."

A confused Naomi continued to look at Marquise as if he'd lost his mind. How had their conversation gone completely left so fast?

"Marq, you can't be serious?"

"Dead serious," he reiterated.

"So what you're saying is not to let him see his kids? That they don't need to go over there or communicate with him at all?" Naomi attempted to understand. Right now she just couldn't believe what she was hearing.

"What I'm saying is as long as that nigga thinks he can get out of his body with you, he don't need to be around none of y'all! You said he acted like he wanted to put his hands on you, right? Well I'm tellin' you there won't be a next time for his ass! Don't go nowhere near that nigga, your old crib, or nothin' associated with him! I'm not fuckin playing, Nao!" Marquise declared as he stood up and walked out of the room.

Naomi continued to sit on the bed in shock. What in the hell had just happened? It was one thing to be going through things with Tyree, her best friend, and even her father. But to have an issue with Marquise was something entirely different.

She was beyond exhausted and no longer had the energy to discuss the day's events. All she wanted to do was go to sleep, and prayed that tomorrow would be much different.

CHAPTER 11

Tyree: *I'm sorry, Naomi.*

Tyree: *Please answer I'm sick as hell without you and the kids here.*

Tyree*: I fucked up... but I need to see my kids. Please I'm beggin' you.*

Tyree: *They are all I have left, Naomi.*

The next day had proven to be just as eventful as the previous day. To say that she was stressed was a complete understatement. Every time her phone rang or a text came through, she dreaded taking a peek considering it may have been him.

Her fingers wavered over the text screen which held messages between her and Marquise. He'd left early that morning without saying goodbye and she hadn't heard from him since. She wanted to text him, but her feelings were hurt. He'd snapped on her and hadn't apologized for it either. That didn't sit well with her no matter how much she tried to ignore the elephant in the room.

"Mommy? Did you forget that I have ballet tomorrow?" Josie asked while entering the bedroom.

Of course she'd forgot. She couldn't even remember what she ate for dinner last night, let alone her kids schedules.

"Uh, no sweetie, I didn't forget. Ballet is Monday and Wednesday, right?" Naomi responded.

"Yes, that's right, but I don't have my tutu or shoes," she added.

It dawned on her that she hadn't been to the house since the incident. None of her kid's belongings besides the contents of their suitcases, were here at Marquise's house.

"Chris has baseball tomorrow too, Mommy. He doesn't have his practice clothes or glove," Josie pointed out.

"Don't worry, baby. Mommy will make sure you guys are ready for tomorrow, alright?" Naomi declared.

"Okay," Josie replied before running off to go find her brother for another round of hide and seek.

Thoughts of Marquise's last words crossed her mind...

"What I'm saying is as long as that nigga thinks he can get out of his body with you, he don't need to be around none of y'all! You said he acted like he wanted to put his hands on you, right? Well I'm tellin' you there won't be a next time for his ass! Don't go nowhere near that nigga, your old crib, or nothin' associated with him! I'm not fuckin' playin', Nao!"

She nervously chewed her bottom lip as she contemplated her next move. Even though Marq had warned her about going back to the house, Naomi felt as if she had no other choice. She had to make her kids feel as normal as possible, and continuing their daily routine was key to the process.

Fuck it!

"Kids, put on your shoes! We're going to visit Grandma!" Naomi yelled.

"Alright!" Christopher responded.

Naomi couldn't help but to feel like she was playing with fire, but she had to do what she had to do.

***

Naomi drove towards her old house as a wave of nausea passed through her. She knew for a fact that Tyree wasn't home so as far as running in to him, she knew she was in the clear. But it still didn't make her feel any better. She knew that the minute she stepped foot in that house, the memories of what she'd witnessed would come back to haunt her.

She pulled into the driveway and turned her car off before slowly opening her car door. She tightly held her house key in the palm of her hand as she turned it over and over out of nervousness.

"Come on, Naomi, you can do this. In and out," she said aloud in an effort to give herself a pep talk.

She took a deep breath and finally climbed out of the car. With hurried steps, she made her way to the front door before using her key to unlock it. She turned the doorknob, opened the front door, and stepped inside being sure to close it behind her. She looked around at a home she no longer recognized.

From the old pizza boxes and articles of Tyree's clothing randomly thrown around the house. The house was in complete disarray.

This nigga is losing it!

Naomi shook her head as she ran up the stairs, taking two at a time until she reached Josie's bedroom. She quickly grabbed her ballet stuff, clothes, and anything else she felt her daughter would miss living without. She then went to Christopher's room and did the same thing. She paused outside of the bedroom that she'd once shared with Tyree for a moment, as she contemplated going inside to grab some more of her things.

She quickly decided against it before jogging back down the stairs to retrieve a suitcase from the front closet. She quickly threw everything inside and then went back into each one of their bedrooms to make sure she grabbed everything. Once she was satisfied, she came back down stairs and zipped up the suitcase. She walked back to the front door and opened it. She took one last look around before locking and closing the door behind her.

Naomi rolled the suitcase down the driveway and put it inside of her trunk. She slammed it closed and climbed back inside of her car. She finally released the breath she'd been holding as she started her car and bagged out of the driveway. She drove towards Marquise's condo to put the kids' things away before taking the long drive back to her parents' house.

Ring! Ring! Ring!

Naomi rummaged through her purse while using the other to steer. She grabbed her phone and looked at the caller I.D. It was a number she didn't recognize so she answered, just in case it was Marq trying to get in contact with her.

"Hello?" Naomi answered.

"Naomi? Naomi, I am so sorry! I just need you to understand that—" Erin blabbed.

Naomi immediately hung up once she realized who was calling. Once again she was fuming, because, no matter what she said, this girl just didn't get it. They would never ever be friends again and there was nothing she could say to ever make her even consider forgiving her. Erin was foul, point, black, period.

Naomi felt herself getting frustrated as she pulled into the parking lot. She was trying her hardest to see the brighter side of things these days, but no matter how hard she tried, she just kept getting slapped in the face. She just wished that both Erin and Tyree would let things be.

She popped her trunk before quickly hopping out of the car to grab the suitcase. She closed the truck behind her and walked to the entrance of the building before taking the elevator to their floor. She stepped off of the elevator and grabbed her key from her pocket to open the front door. Naomi slid her key inside of the lock and opened the door, as she dragged the heavy suitcase inside before closing the door behind her. She set her key on the counter and headed straight for their bedrooms to put their things away.

As she turned the corner and stepped inside, she was startled to find Marquise standing near the wall closest to the window in Christopher's room.

"Shit, Marq, you scared me!" Naomi admitted as she placed her hand over her chest.

Marquis turned around with a smirk on his face. "Well, hello to you too, Nao."

Naomi couldn't help but smile. Marquise's sexy smile could light up any room.

"I meant to say what are you doing here? I didn't expect you to be home until later?" she corrected.

"I wanted to do something to make the kids feel more at home. I know yesterday was rough on them, so I got some stuff to decorate their rooms."

Naomi felt her heart melt at his words. Here she was thinking he was mad at her, when the entire time he'd been out shopping. For the first time since entering the room, she took a look around. She stared in amazement at all of the decorations that he'd placed on the walls. Marquise had created a sports theme inside of the room with different hues of blue and green, which were Christopher's favorite colors.

"So what you think?"

"I think it's perfect. He's going to love it!" Naomi confirmed.

She loved the fact that her man was going all out to make them happy.

"I was going to do Josie's room next. Wanna help me?" he asked after hanging a picture on the wall.

"Sure, I'd love to."

Marquise walked towards Naomi and wrapped his arms around her. He kissed her forehead before lightly kissing her lips.

"What's in the suitcase?"

Naomi's entire body tensed up. She'd been so caught up in the work that Marquise had done, that she'd totally forgotten her reason for coming to the house in the first place.

"Oh, uh, just some of the kids' things that I need to put away, that's all," Naomi countered.

As if sensing her hesitance, Marquise continued to observe her odd behavior.

Marquise released her and took a step back while looking around the room. He searched with his eyes until he laid eyes on the object that he was looking for: *Christopher's suitcase.*

Marquise looked at her with pure anger and Naomi felt a blush creep up her neck.

"Naomi, tell me you didn't do what the fuck I think you did?"

Naomi bit her bottom lip before saying, "Yes, I did go over to the house, but only to get the rest of their things. Josie and Christopher both have activities tomorrow and they wouldn't have been able to participate without them."

Marquise shook his head as he stared at her in disbelief.

"And you don't think you could have called me to pick up whatever it was they needed from the store before coming home?"

"No, I didn't at the time, besides, why waste money? I went there and got everything while he was gone. I swear I was in and out."

"You just don't get it, do you? You did the exact opposite of what I said after I said it, which was less than twenty-four hours ago! What the fuck is wrong with you?" Marquise yelled.

Naomi truly understood his frustration, but what she wasn't going to do was be chastised like she was a child.

"Marquise, do not yell at me! I wasn't trying to piss you off or defy you! I only wanted to do what was best for the kids. Let me remind you that I have been looking out for me and my kids for a long time now, so don't expect me to call you for every little thing! I know you're mad at me, but I'm not a damn child!" Naomi responded.

She felt her own blood begin to boil.

"Naomi, you really pushin' my fuckin' buttons right now. It ain't about you defying me, it's about your ass putting yourself in another situation that I'm just tryna protect you from!"

"I'm not some damn damsel in distress, Marq!" she countered as she stormed out of the room and into the living room with Marquise close on her heels.

"Nah, you not, but you so damn used to being the man and woman in your old relationship, that you got me fucked up! See, it's certain shit I ain't gone stand for and you disregarding me like what I gotta say don't mean shit, not gone fly with me!"

Naomi took a step back to observe his demeanor. She'd seen this look in his eyes before; she'd hurt his pride.

"Marq, what do you want from me?" she cried out of frustration.

"What I want, Naomi, is for you to realize I meant what the fuck I said! Ain't shit keepin' me from killin' that nigga right now. I don't give a fuck about him being their father either, so you can save that shit!" Marq yelled while looking her right in the eyes.

Naomi attempted to speak, but was cut off as he began to speak again.

"Furthermore, don't insult my intelligence. You know damn well there ain't nothin' that y'all need that I won't take care of. You fuckin' with a real man, Nao, and you need to get used to that, plain and simple. I thought we was on the same page, but I see we ain't," Marq clarified while shaking his head and heading for the door.

"Marquise! It's really not this damn serious. Tyree is their father whether you like it or not, and keeping them from him is only going to hurt the kids," she stated.

"That nigga already done enough damage to scar them for a lifetime if they really knew the truth, yet you standing here defending this nigga? Tuh! Look, I'm gone. Don't wait up," Marquise said before slamming the door behind him.

Naomi scrubbed her hand down her face. She ran her fingers through her hair before looking up at the ceiling. Anger was flowing through her like a wave of electricity and there was nothing she could do about it. Marquise and her had just had one of the worst arguments ever and she didn't know how they were going to fix it.

She sat down on the couch and held her head in her hands. They simply did not agree when it came to the kids and the situation surrounding their father. Although Tyree was a shitty husband to her, in Naomi's opinion, that had nothing to do with his parenting. As far as she was concerned, she'd never grown up without a father and neither would her children.

Marq was tripping. She wasn't going to interfere with Tyree being a father and if he couldn't understand that, she didn't know what would become of their relationship.

CHAPTER 12

How could she have been so damn disrespectful?

Marquise just didn't understand why Naomi wasn't respecting his wishes. As her man, it was his duty to always look after her and have her best interest at heart.

That's all he ever continued to do for her, but it seemed like she was too busy always trying to be Miss Independent and not actually respecting their relationship. They were together as one and that meant that as a couple they did things together.

However, Naomi just didn't seem to get that. She was more concerned with doing whatever suited her without letting Marquise know about it.

Was she high?

She already knew exactly how Marquise got down. She knew he wasn't one to play with, but here she was playing games.

Of course Marquise was pissed that Naomi had the audacity to go behind his back and do the very thing he told her not to do. He didn't want her going back to her old crib with Tyree and collecting the kids' old stuff.

Marquise already promised to take the kids shopping to buy them whatever they needed and wanted. He was willing to do anything for them, but how was he supposed to do that if Naomi didn't even give him a damn chance to?

Now they weren't talking. Things were tense and awkward between the two of them. And as much as Marquise wanted to be good with Naomi again, he wasn't about to apologize. Apologize for what? If anything, the only person who deserved an apology was him from her, for being so rude, disobedient and disrespectful. He was just going to continue to ignore her until she came to her senses.

There was no point of Marquise dwelling about his argument with Naomi when something more troubling was deep on his mind.

The mysterious caller was starting to get on his last nerve now and he really wished that the caller would say something to him instead of being a pussy all the time. He was tired of picking up the call, asking who it was and hearing the call suddenly end. He just wanted to know who it was and what the hell they wanted.

Marquise didn't even have a clue who it could be and he hoped to God that it wasn't someone from his past that he truly hated. Only Lord knows what he would do once he laid eyes on them.

Marquise was suddenly distracted by his vibrating phone that was currently sitting on his lap. He picked his phone up only to see Blaze's incoming message.

Took the offer from Sergio, niggas.

A few months back, the connect that provided Marquise's squad with some of the finest Colombian weed known to man and all the other drugs they ever required, had offered Blaze a job. A job as his own connect for their Knight Nation. Sergio was retiring and he wanted Blaze to take his place as one of the most well-known connects in the United States. Now it looked like Blaze had decided to take the offer.

Kareem: *Congrats, nigga!*

Marquise: *Congrats, fool!*

Blaze: *Thanks, y'all. Wish me luck on tellin' Nika though.*

Kareem: *What, she don't know?*

Blaze: *Nah, not yet.*

Marquise: *Good luck.*

Kareem: *Gooooood luck.*

Blaze: *Thanks fools.*

Marquise could only wish Blaze the best of luck and hoped that Anika was happy for her man. But Marquise couldn't help but guess that Anika wouldn't be happy knowing her man was getting even deeper into the dope game. And Marquise guessed right because within a few hours, Blaze texted the group chat back.

Blaze: *Told Anika. Went crazy.*

Marquise: *So I take it she don't want you bein' the connect?*

Blaze: *Nah.*

Marquise: *Where you at now?*

Blaze: *I had to leave the crib. She was trippin' and I couldn't take it anymore.*

Kareem: *Where you going?*

Blaze: *My club. I'm not tryna hear her shout no more.*

Kareem: *Man... At least yo' girl still tell you how she feels and shit. Mine won't even talk to me.*

Marquise: *She gon' come round soon, nigga, don't worry.*

Kareem: *I don't know... I feel like it might be ova between us.*

Blaze: *It ain't. She was here this afternoon, talkin' to Anika 'bout you.*

Kareem: *Oh word?*

Blaze: *Yeah, she still loves yo' dumb ass.*

Kareem: *So why won't she talk to me already? Or answer any of my calls.*

Blaze: *She just needs space.*

Marquise: *Probably just tryna heal. You know the usual female shit they be doin' all the time. She gon' come round.*

Kareem: *And if she don't?*

Marquise: *Then you gon' have to fight for yo' relationship.*

Blaze: *Yeah, what he said.*

***

Erin took a sip of her vodka bottle before chucking it back down onto her table.

What she didn't understand was why Naomi just wouldn't hear her out?

She had done what she had done for her and nobody else. All she ever wanted was for her best friend to be happy. Was that a crime now? She just didn't understand why Naomi was taking this shit to heart?

Yeah, she had slept with Tyree numerous times, but Naomi never really wanted him in the first place. She was always complaining about how she wanted Marquise alone and now she had Marquise alone, so why wasn't Naomi thanking her?

After all she had done for her, Erin was repaid with a simple block button every time she used a different number to get through to Naomi.

Ding!

Erin looked down at her phone that sat in the middle of her thighs and picked it up with a frown.

Ty: *So that's it? You come over to see me last night, drunk, fuck me all night and then bounce in the morning?*

Erin rolled her eyes with disgust as she remembered what she had done with Tyree last night. And here she was, drinking again.

Ty: *Stop ignoring me, Erin. I need to know.*

Erin: *Need to know what?*

Ty: *Is you with me or what?*

Erin: *Nigga, nah.*

Erin: *Go away and leave me alone.*

Ty: *Are you for real right now? You telling me to leave you alone, but you weren't sayin' that yesterday when you were choking and spitting all over this dick.*

Erin: *It's over. I'm done. Delete my number.*

Ty: *I can't!*

Erin: *You can. Goodbye.*

Ty: *I love you.*

Erin didn't even bother replying to his last message. She was hoping that he never told her that he loved her. She was hoping that she never saw those words or heard those words from him. But now she had and now she was annoyed.

What was she supposed to say to that shit?

She knew for a fact that she didn't love him, but she did have strong feelings for him. Whether they were strong or not, whatever they had going on was stopping. She was no longer messing around with him! All she wanted was her best friend back.

She missed Naomi dearly and just really wished that they were back on speaking terms, because she couldn't take not being able to call her to just talk like they used to.

Ty: *I love you, Erin Jones, and I want to be with you.*

Ty: *I want us to be together.*

Ty: *I know what we had was lust at the start, but I've grown to love you now. Seriously, Erin.*

Ty: *Stop ignoring me and tell me you love me too.*

Erin: *I don't love you.*

Ty: *What?*

Erin: *I said I don't love you. I never have and I never will. I love my best friend and that's who I need to get back into my life and in order for me to do that, you need to stay away from me.*

Ty: *You're the one always running back to me, Erin.*

Erin: *Well no more of that bullshit then. Naomi hasn't forgiven me, even though I've tried to explain to her a million times that I did this shit for her. I did it all for her.*

Ty: *What type of "best friend" sleeps with her best friend's husband and says she did it as a favor? As a way to help her? Are you well? That isn't normal shit. People don't just go around sleeping with husbands to help others.*

Ty: *Just admit you wanted me from the start.*

Erin: *I never ever wanted you. I hated you. I just wanted Naomi to be happy and in order for her to be happy, she had to be with Marquise. Not you.*

Ty: *You're so stupid. It's like you're obsessed with her.*

Erin didn't get this fool. One minute he claimed he loved her, the next minute he was insulting her calling her stupid.

Erin: *I just wanted what was best for her and you were clearly not best for her.*

Ty: *But by wanting what was best for her, how is that benefiting your life in any shape or form? You're just crazy.*

Erin: *And you're just a lazy, good for nothing fool that's going to forever be alone.*

Ty: *Forever alone? Nah, I could get Naomi back within a heartbeat.*

Erin couldn't help but chuckle loudly as she stared down at conversation with Tyree. Was this guy retarded or something?

Ty: *She still loves me.*

Erin: *You must be high if you believe that she still loves you. She wants absolutely nothing to do with you. Before you know it she'll be asking for a divorce and marrying her new man who treats her a hundred times better than you ever could. You idiot! Keep living a dumb life while Naomi enjoys her man and the family they're going to build together, with your kids, nigga.*

Ty: *Fuck you.*

Erin: *Uh-uh, you can't do that anymore nigga. Like I said before, we're done!*

Erin: *Have a good day all by yourself :)*

***

Naomi sighed deeply as she tried her hardest to fight the tears trying to escape her eyes. She continued to dish her babies' food out and kept her eyes away from Marquise's, trying to avoid his hard gaze.

"You guys miss me as much as I missed y'all?" Marquise asked them sweetly.

"Yeah!" Josie exclaimed with excitement.

"Yeah, I did too!" Chris stated happily. "Do you still have that basketball game on your phone for me?"

"Of course I do, lil' man," Marquise responded with a smile. "I couldn't delete it when I know how hard you worked to get to level ten."

Naomi cracked a small smile appreciating the effort Marquise was making with her kids. She was glad that he wasn't taking his anger towards her, out on them. She remembered the days Tyree used to do that shit.

While they ate dinner, the kids and Marquise talked, catching up all together while Naomi decided to stay right out of their conversation. She didn't want to join in, but she did chuckle and smile a few times.

Naomi wasn't sure when or how her and Marquise were going to start talking again, but she hoped that it happened sooner than later. She didn't like it when they weren't on speaking terms.

Things were awkward and tense between them and she just wanted things to be normal.

Hopefully that normal came real soon.

Ring! Ring! Ring!

Naomi's head shot up from her half eaten plate and she looked straight at Marquise's phone that sat on the mahogany table.

She carefully observed as he looked down at the caller I.D. with a frown before deciding to pick it up.

"Don't hang up," Marquise quickly blurted out. "Who is this? I'm getting real tired of these silly games you keep playin'."

The kids kept quiet and drank their juice while Marquise's phone call dominated the sound of the room.

Silly games?

What was he talking about? Naomi's curiosity only continued to grow as she watched Marquise on the phone. Her eyes connected with his hazel eyes and he just kept them on her. Naomi didn't bother lifting her eyes off his.

"Just tell me who you are," Marquise demanded firmly.

Naomi continued to watch as Marquise's firm, stern facial expression suddenly changed to surprise. Then his eyes began to widen with fear.

Naomi didn't care that they weren't talking. She still wanted to know what was going on with her man. But before she could ask him, he was quickly up and out of his seat with his phone still pressed to his ear as he listened to his phone call.

Naomi knew she definitely needed to find out what was going on.

CHAPTER 13

"What?"

"It's me, Marquise," she voiced quietly. "Your mother."

"No it fuckin' ain't," Marquise snapped, slamming his bedroom door behind him. "Who is this?"

"It's me, Marquise," she repeated. "Your mother, Rose."

"My mother became dead to me when she abandoned me when I was nothing but a teenager and had no one else to depend on but my older brother, who is now dead because of her stupid, fucking decisions. So I'll ask you again, who the fuck is this?"

"I'm sorry for what... for all I did, Marquise," she commented, ignoring Marquise's angry words from before. "I never was supposed to leave you for him, but you see he promised me the world... He promised me everything I ever wanted, but I couldn't have it if I still had you and your brother. That's why I lef—"

"No!" Marquise barked, cutting her off. "You left because you ain't nothin' but a thot ass bitch that wanted to go off with a rich man that felt absolutely nothin' for you! That nigga never wanted you because he loved you, he was just using you. And you allowed him to!"

Marquise could feel his eyes becoming heavy and starting to burn the more he continued to think about what she had done to him in the past. All these years and he still hadn't healed from all the pain that she had caused him. It still hurt him deeply that she had ditched him because of a man that had a big house, big cars, and all the money she wished she could have.

She was nothing but a whore to him.

"Marquise, you're still my son and I'm still your mother. I'm sorry I kept on calling... I wasn't sure what to say every time you picked up. When I first heard your voice I just froze, forgetting all the things I had already planned to say to yo—"

"Look, I don't fuckin' care! You're not my mom, so dead that shit right now. Like I said before, my mom is dead to me now and I never want to see her or hear from her ever again. She can run right back to the nigga that had her running head over hills for him and leave me alone. I don't want or need her in my life anymore. A'ight?"

"Marq—"

Marquise immediately hung up the call and blocked her number. He fought back the tears trying to leave his eyes right now. He didn't want to cry over that woman. The same woman that had hurt him in the worst way in the past.

He didn't even understand how she had gotten hold of his number. It didn't make any sense to him at all. Why was she suddenly trying to contact him and get back into his life?

Marquise didn't want a single thing to do with her. He would just prefer it if she left him alone. She seemed perfectly fine with leaving him for her rich, bourgeois boyfriend all those years ago, so she could run right back and stay with him. Marquise hated her with all his heart and soul. He was sure that was the way things were going to stay.

She was dead to him.

***

Even though Naomi badly wanted to question Marquise about what was going on with him, she didn't have the courage to. Every time she tried to start a conversation, she felt her throat closing up and no words sounding out. Why was she so nervous to talk to her man all of a sudden? Why were they having this petty little quarrel? And why in the hell weren't they trying to sort it out?

Naomi didn't have the answer to any of her questions right now, so she decided that the best thing for her to do now that the kids were tucked in their beds and sleeping peacefully, was for her to do the exact same.

Ever since Marquise had taken his call at the dinner table and left, he silently came back, ate the rest of his meal, and then left the house. He had told the kids he was going out for a quick drive, his way of indirectly letting Naomi know where he was going and then went.

Now Naomi was in bed all by herself, feeling like shit. Tiny tears slowly left her cheeks as she thought about how much she wanted Marquise in bed with her right now, with his strong arms around her and him just kissing on her neck as they both fell asleep together. She just wanted them to be back on speaking terms again. Was that so hard to ask for?

Ding!

Naomi quickly reached across to the lamp stand for her vibrating phone, praying it was the person she really wanted to speak to right now. But it wasn't. Instead it was the devil himself.

Ty: *Naomi, please... I just need to see my kids. That's all I'm askin'.*

Reluctantly, Naomi looked down at the text and just stared at it. She couldn't keep her kids away from their father. It just wasn't right and she knew that sooner or later, she was going to need to let them see their father.

Naomi: *Alright...*

Naomi: *You can see them tomorrow. I'll text you a time later on.*

Ty: *Thank you so much and I'm really sorry about what I did.*

Naomi took one last glance at Tyree's text and decided to lock her iPhone screen and place it back on the lamp stand. There was no point in this petty shit she was doing anymore. It was just best she let the kids see their dad. That way they wouldn't be begging and constantly pleading to see him.

Naomi couldn't help but cry as she thought back to her argument with Marquise. She was being such a pussy for crying right now, but she couldn't help it. That's the effect that Marquise had on her emotions. That's how much she loved him.

Five minutes later, Naomi was finally getting a chance to catch up on some much needed sleep. But it was only half an hour later when she felt sweet kisses in between her thighs that she suddenly woke up.

"Marq..."

Naomi shyly looked down between her legs only to stare into those mesmerizing hazel eyes that knew all the right ways to turn her on.

"Sorry I woke you up, bae. But I didn't want to go to sleep without us talkin' again," Marquise explained simply, shifting his body upwards so that he could rest on Naomi's stomach. "I'm sorry for how I spoke to you the other day, it was out of order I admit that, but you know exactly how I feel about that nigga and all he did to you."

Naomi sighed softly, finally happy that they were back on speaking terms again. She didn't care about what they talked about, just as long as she could hear his voice speaking to her.

"I know, Marq..."

"You been crying, baby?" Marquise suddenly questioned her, lifting a hand to her cheek and wiping off her dry tears.

Naomi slowly nodded, feeling more tears trying to burst through again. What was up with her and this crying?

"Why, sweetheart? Was it me?" The guilty expression plastered upon his handsome face right now had Naomi's heart melting. She loved how much he cared about her.

"I was just upset that we weren't talking, that's all," Naomi stated. "I'm okay and I'm glad we're talking now."

"See, Nao, we can't start that petty miscommunication shit. I don't wanna be one of those couples that go to sleep with their problems unsolved. We need to communicate 24/7, that's it," Marquise voiced seriously, rubbing gently on Naomi's cheek. "I love you and I don't ever wanna see you cry because of some bullshit that I did."

"I love you, too, Marquise, and I just want us to be good. I understand how you feel about Tyree and I won't argue with you about that. But you know he's still the father of my children. He's still gonna be in my life no matter what and that's just the way things will forever be."

"I know, Nao… I guess I just need to get used to that shit from now on," Marquise said coolly. "It'll take some time, but I promise to get used to it."

Naomi really appreciated the fact that Marquise was going to try his hardest to tolerate Tyree. She knew how hard that was going to be for him, especially since he hated Tyree very much, but Naomi appreciated the effort he was going to make.

"Who was the person that called you earlier on, Marq?"

"At the dinner table?"

She nodded before replying, "Yeah, who was it?"

"My mother."

Naomi's eyes widened with surprise.

She knew all about Marquise's mother and what she had done to Marquise when he was just a teenager, age fifteen. When he needed her the most in his life, going through a very hard adolescent time, she was more concerned about having her fun.

She abandoned Marquise and his older brother, leaving them with no money, no support, and no food. She simply told them that it was time for them to step up to the plate as men and to fend for themselves. She left them with absolutely nothing and was much more focused on chasing after her rich boyfriend who only wanted her for one thing.

Naomi listened as Marquise explained that he had been having a series of mysterious calls all throughout last month and it was only until today that the mysterious caller had finally been revealed as his mother. She wanted his forgiveness, but Marquise wasn't so sure he could give it to her.

"Maybe you should just hear her out some more, Marq... She's your mother," Naomi softly suggested.

"Nah, fuck that," he snapped. "She was my mother when she left me for that nigga, right? Now she's completely dead to me."

"Baby, I know you're mad but remember you forgave me, right? When I lied to you."

"But that situation is completely different from this one, Nao," Marquise protested. "You didn't leave me. Yes, you lied, but you stayed with me regardless because you love me. She didn't stay with me, she left me."

He had a point, but Naomi still figured it wouldn't hurt for him to give his mother a chance to explain why she had done what she did.

"I still think you should consider hearing her out, baby. It could really help you heal from that time in your life, really let it go, you know?"

"Hmm... You probably right, bae, but I need to think about it. Really think about it," Marquise concluded before moving closer to Naomi to gently peck her lips. "I missed you."

"I missed you, too."

"Promise we never gon' do that ignoring shit again."

"I promise, daddy."

Marquise leaned back into Naomi's soft lips before latching their lips together and beginning to seductively suck on her bottom lip, before tongue kissing her down. His hands also began to wrap around her waist so he could pull her closer to him and have his hands on her body while they passionately kissed.

But in between their deep kiss, Marquise couldn't help but contemplate on something that had actually been bothering him for a quite a while. He knew for a fact that he couldn't keep thinking about it without letting Naomi know what was on his mind. He just hoped that she took it well and didn't want her to think that he was trying to pressure her. He just wanted things to move smoothly and efficiently between them. And he believed that by her doing this, things were going to be much smoother and easier.

"Nao," Marquise spoke up as he pulled his lips off hers.

"What's up?" Naomi sighed, leaning into Marquise's neck, gently kissing on his warm skin.

"I was wondering if you would be willing to consider something."

"What's... that?" Naomi quietly queried, focused on kissing and pleasing him.

"Well..." Marquise couldn't help but smile at Naomi's attempts to turn him on and he couldn't lie, it was definitely working. "I was wondering if you would be considering..."

"Considering?"

"A divorce."

CHAPTER 14

A divorce?

Naomi knew that this situation would be occurring soon, she just didn't think it would be coming so soon.

A divorce...

That's what Marquise wanted from her and she knew that if she continued to avoid it, he would only drive harder and harder onto her.

A divorce!

If someone had come to Naomi a year ago and told her that she would start cheating on her husband only for him to later cheat on her, she would have told them that they were a damn liar. Back then she thought that she loved Tyree with all her heart and soul and that there was absolutely no other man she wanted except him.

But then she met Marquise Lewis, who managed to sweep her completely off her feet. He had changed the entire course of her life forever. She thought that she was going to be with Tyree forever, but that thought had completely died. She really had to make a decision on whether or not she was filing for a divorce.

A divorce.

Naomi hadn't bothered telling Marquise where she was taking the kids early in the morning. She just quickly dropped them off with Tyree, not bothering to go inside and see the look on his face once seeing that they had been reunited.

Ty: *What time you coming back to pick them up?*

Naomi: *4pm.*

Ty: *Cool.*

It was now 1:35pm and Naomi knew that now more than ever she needed somebody to talk to. That person was the only woman in her life that she loved so much, the only woman she would ever die for.

Her mother.

When finally arriving to meet her mother at a local restaurant in downtown Atlanta, she hugged and kissed her before taking a seat opposite her.

"Thanks for agreeing to meet me here, mom," Naomi thanked her happily.

"It's okay, baby," her mother responded lovingly. "I know you don't want to be anywhere near the house right now because of your foolish father... But hey, at least being here gives us a chance to really catch up, right?"

"Right," Naomi said with a confident nod. "We definitely have a lot to catch up on... I could really use your advice right now, Mom."

"With what, honey? You know whatever you need I'm here for you always."

"Marquise wants me to divorce Tyree," Naomi explained.

"Okay... And what's the issue? Don't you want that too?"

"I do, but... Mom, I just never thought that this would be happening to me," Naomi voiced. "I never would have imagined myself having to file for a divorce from my husband. I didn't even think I could love no other man except Tyree, and then Marq came along."

"So what you're trying to tell me is that you're scared? Is that it?" her mother queried curiously with a raised brow. "You're scared of the divorce?"

Naomi sheepishly nodded before answering, "What if Marquise and I don't work out, Mom? Who is gonna want me then? I'm getting older and I can't be jumping from man to man."

"What are you talking about, Naomi? From what I've seen, Marquise really loves you with all his heart and soul. He won't ever leave you."

Naomi could only sigh with misery at the doubtful thoughts constantly flying around her head. She blamed her father for these thoughts. It was his words she couldn't stop thinking about.

"I don't need to know him, Naomi, because I know men like him! You had a family, silly girl! You gave that up for a damn thug who is going to drag you down into the gutter right along with him. You'll end up so far down that neither of us will be able to get you out!"

She blamed him completely.

***

Marquise placed the bottle of whiskey in the center of the wooden table where the boys all sat around, and placed the three glasses in front of everyone.

Blaze was the first one to grab the bottle and pour himself a large amount that reached the tip of his glass. Then he lifted the glass to his lips and swung it all down in one whole chug.

"Damn, nigga," Kareem called out to him. "Slow down, we just got here."

"He needs it," Marquise stated simply. "We all do with the shit we been going through."

"All 'cause of these females... Man, I'm sick of feelin' like this," Kareem explained. "Sadie still hasn't come 'round despite all the space I've given her, and I just don't know what the fuck to do anymore."

"How long has it been since y'all last spoke?" Blaze queried suddenly.

"More than two weeks," Kareem stated sadly. "She won't answer a nigga's calls or reply to my texts. She only replied once when I told her that I can't live wit'out her."

"What she say?" Marquise queried.

"She said 'Die then'."

"Damn that's cold," Marquise exclaimed with a scoff.

"Ice cold," Blaze mumbled as he reached for the whiskey bottle again.

"I've given her all the space she wants and she still don't wan' a nigga? We can't keep doin' this shit. We either togetha or we not."

"You love her, right?" Marquise asked.

Kareem quickly nodded.

"Then just give her some more space. She's probably missin' yo' ass and she gon' come 'round soon. Don't worry, just leave her alone for some more," Marquise advised simply.

"I hope you right, nigga, I'm tired of waitin'. I want her back already, I miss her."

"What happened wit' you and Anika, B'?"

Blaze looked up at Marquise's curious hazel eyes, only to sigh deeply before responding, "We had an argument about the job offer from the connect," he began with a frown. "I decided to give her space, so I left to go to my club. Candi came to see me and before a nigga knew it, she was on her knees suckin' me off and titty fuckin' me."

"What?!" Marquise immediately burst into laughter.

"What's funny, fool?" Blaze wasn't liking the way he was suddenly laughing at him. What the hell was funny?

"It's the way yo' ass said titty..." His words trailed off as he burst into laughter again. Marquise couldn't help it. The shit sounded funny.

"That's not even the best part," Blaze snapped tensely. "Anika came in once I had managed to stop her. Then she was rushin' back home and packin' her shit up."

"Did you not try and stop her?" Kareem asked.

"Of course, I tried to stop her, but we ended up arguin' even more and she just pissed me off completely. We weren't gettin' anywhere, so I let her go, and we ain't talked since."

"Damn... That's cold," Marquise commented.

"Ice cold," Kareem said. "So what'chu finna do now?"

"Just givin' her ass some space."

"And if she doesn't come 'round?" Kareem curiously queried.

"She gon' come 'round," Blaze responded. "She know we supposed to be togetha. She know how much I love her and she know how much she loves me. I'ma just give her some space and hope for the best. There ain't no point in me forcin' her to come back, she gotta do that shit on her own."

"Yeah, I guess you right, nigga," Kareem agreed.

"Compared to all y'all niggas, my problem seems like shit."

"What, you and Naomi, right?" Blaze asked.

"Yeah, yeah... She found out that her best friend and her husband were fuckin' 'round behind her back. So she been stayin' 'round mine, her kids are with us too now, but she's always fuckin' cryin' and I just don't know what the hell to do."

"It's probably a huge shock to her now, knowin' that they were sneakin' 'round her back. That's probably why she keeps cryin'," Kareem suggested.

"She found them fuckin'," Marquise revealed.

"Woah... what?" Blaze couldn't believe it.

"On their shared bed," Marquise continued. "They got kids together, but they went to summer camp for two weeks, and Naomi decided to spend the two weeks with me. When she came to see me, I told her I was taking her away for a few days. So she decided that she didn't have the right clothes and shit. I took her to her crib the next day, waited for her to get her shit and she came out in tears. Her best friend had followed her out, tryin' to explain shit, and her husband came out too."

"And what did you do?" Kareem questioned him suspiciously.

"Wait, huh? How you know I did somethin'?"

"We know you did somethin'. Ain't no way you just stayed in that fuckin' car and watched," Blaze announced. "What yo' ass do?"

"Of course I did somethin'!" Marquise exclaimed with a grin. "How could I not? She been tryin' to come to a decision about who she was goin' to choose and I just knew it was gon' be me. So I got out the car, opened the door for her and when that nigga saw me, he started askin' the dumbest questions and tellin' her to get out the car. Then he called her a whore. I lost it after that."

"You fucked him up?"

"Yup," Marquise stated happily. "You know how I get down, B'. I don't like niggas disrespectin' what belongs to me. So I had to teach his ass a lesson. End of story. But only for a bit though, Naomi stopped me."

"Awww man," Kareem groaned. "Why didn't you call us up? That would have been fun to watch."

"Fun?" Blaze's brow rose up with surprise. "Now you know damn well we would have got involved, 'Reem."

"Hmm... Yeah, probably."

"But yeah, she's left him now and now she's wit' me," Marquise declared.

"Are you happy?" Kareem questioned his boy curiously.

"Kinda... I'll be happy when she finally divorces his ass though."

"Well, at least you got somethin' good goin' on compared to 'Reem and I," Blaze said. "We just gotta pray that things get better in our relationships."

"And they will, niggas, don't worry 'bout it. Just give them the space, they love you both, they'll come running," Marquise advised before deciding to switch the subject. "What we need to be worryin' 'bout is Leek and Jamal."

"They still hidin'," Kareem stated. "They gon' come out soon though. They can't be hidin' foreva."

"I already told y'all niggas 'bout my promise to Nika, right?"

Both Kareem and Marquise nodded.

"Yeah, we remember it, B', don't you worry. Besides, with the attorney helpin' us, I'on think we'll need to even kill Jamal," Marquise explained.

"And our real main focus is just endin' all this bullshit once and for all. No more of these fools comin' for us, we ain't got the time for it anymore," Kareem added.

"Exactly," Blaze agreed. "It's time for us to just focus on the future. If Anika wants me to leave the game soon, then I gotta be ready to leave. I can't be beefin' with niggas that aren't doin' anythin' but causin' problems. We get rid of them and then we good."

"And if Sadie wants me to do the same, I gotta be ready too."

"Same with Naomi... If our ladies wan' us to go, we gotta leave knowin' the nation is left in good hands."

They all nodded in agreement before lifting their glasses up in the air, toasting to the Knight Nation and the future with their baes.

***

Marquise took a breath as he looked down at his bright screen. He had been thinking about what Naomi had told him to do. To consider hearing his mother out and now that he had really given it some thought, he figured why not?

It didn't mean that things were going to be amazing between them but he definitely deserved an explanation for the bullshit she had done to him. He needed to know why she had just up and left him. Why didn't she love him enough to stay?

His fingers slowly began to move over his screen and before he knew it, he was calling her number on his call log and nervously holding his phone to his ear as he waited for her to pick up.

"Marquise?"

He took another deep breath before responding.

Here goes nothing...

CHAPTER 15

To say Marquise had a lot on his mind was an understatement. He'd spoken to her again, but this time he'd actually listened to what she had to say. His mother was dead wrong for doing what she'd done to him and his brother all those years ago. Anger resonated inside of him and he'd been contemplating what he should do next. So he sat in silence and deep in thought. Her words played inside of his head...

"Marquise, are you there?"

"Yeah, I'm here," he replied with distain.

"Well, how was your day? How are you feeling?" she questioned as she attempted to make small talk.

"Look, I know you want something. So tell me what it is so we can both move on with our lives," he rudely commented.

"Marquise, I don't want anything from you, I swear. All I want to do is see you. It's been years since I have and I'm afraid I wouldn't even recognize my own son if I saw him on the street," she pleaded.

Marquise sighed as he pinched the bridge of his nose. "For what? Why now?"

Rose paused before answering. "Because I want to apologize, but not like this. I want to look you in the eye. There's a lot we need to catch up on and there are some things that you don't know about."

"I'll let you know, but I'm busy right now. I gotta go, so call me later," he declared as he hung up before she could respond.

Now as he replayed the conversation, he was battling with himself internally. He knew he should be more open minded, but his heart wouldn't allow him to. She broke his heart into a million pieces before any woman had the chance to. It was because of her that he'd used women the way he had prior to Naomi. Although he wished he could forget all about the phone call, he knew deep down inside that it would be impossible.

"Marquise, look what I can do!" Josie laughed as she spun around in her ballet slippers. She was twirling from room to room in an attempt to perfect her technique and was so proud of all that she'd accomplished.

"Good job, sweetie," he said without bothering to look up from his phone. He continued to stare at a few text messages that had come through to his phone. After their last conversation, she'd been texting him nonstop. Rose was pleading for a chance to see him.

Rose: *Please, Marquise. I just want to see you.*

Rose: *I'm your mother and I love you. I know I made some bad choices, but I just want to talk to you.*

Rose: *Let's meet one time. If you don't want to see me anymore after that I'll leave you alone for good.*

For the life of him, he didn't understand what she thought she could possibly say that would make any of the shit she pulled okay. However, the thought was weighing heavy on his mind and he was taking Naomi's words to heart. Sure it was easy to ignore her before and act as though she never existed because she'd cut them out of her life all on her own. But, now that she'd resurfaced, it had proven to be difficult. The ball was in his court and he felt weak for even considering her request.

"Marquise, come play the game with me! I almost beat the level!" Christopher yelled while playing his favorite game.

Marquise didn't respond as he continued to look down at his phone. Then suddenly he felt little fingers on his shoulder tapping away for his attention. Marquise looked up to find Josie staring at him with those big, brown eyes and the cutest little smile.

"Can you help me practice my lift? I need to practice before my recital and you promised."

Marquise exhaled at the question and began to look around the room. There were toys randomly scattered throughout the house. Not to mention a laundry hamper was sitting on the couch directly next to Christopher and his bag of unfinished snacks had fell on the floor at his feet.

Naomi walked back into the living room carrying another laundry hamper headed straight for the bedroom.

"Give me a second, baby girl," he finally responded.

He stood up stepping over everything that littered the floor and grabbed the other laundry hamper off of the couch. He then walked into the bedroom to find Naomi folding clothes. He set the hamper on the bed as he observed her.

His frustration was growing by the minute and he didn't understand how she was in such a good mood. The house was in shambles and she'd just cleaned it from top to bottom yesterday. Now she was singing along to Rihanna like it was nothing new to her.

Of course it wasn't. She was a mother and she'd grown accustomed to her routine. She'd learned to live with the ups and downs of motherhood all the while keeping a smile on her face.

"Bae, why you doing all this by yourself instead of askin' for some help?" he questioned with a raised eyebrow.

"I will when I need help," she smiled with a response as she continued to fold.

"Well, it looks like you need help to me," he added as he sat down so that he could sit directly in her line of vision.

A confused Naomi stopped folding to observe his demeanor. He had a frown on his face and appeared to be annoyed, but she didn't understand why.

Crash!

Both Naomi and Marquise turned their attention to the doorway to find Josie standing next to a glass end table where a portrait that was once on the wall was now resting on the floor. The canvas was also torn which made Marquise angry. The portrait was the only thing he had left of his brother and there was no way he would be able to repair it now that it had been damaged so badly.

"Oh, Josie, you in trouble!" Christopher yelled.

"It was an accident. Mommy?" Josie declared.

"Coming, honey," Naomi exclaimed as she continued to look Marquise in the eyes.

"Marquise, I thought we were going to communicate? If there's something going on talk to me, baby," she demanded as she took a seat next to him.

Marquise just stared at her. He was angry for so many reasons that he couldn't openly express to her at this very moment without the kids hearing. Furthermore, he wanted to tell her exactly what he was feeling, but didn't want to hurt her feelings. He had enough problems in his life right now.

There was nothing more to say because Naomi just didn't understand. He felt it was best that he go and get some air. The walls were closing in on him and needed to get away.

"I'm going to go meet the fellas for a minute. I'll be home soon," he said.

Naomi watched as he grabbed his keys and headed straight for the door without saying another word.

***

Marquise sat at the bar between both Kareem and Blaze as he drank yet another shot to calm his nerves. If there was anyone he could trust to give some good advice, it was his boys, and right now that's exactly what he needed. The fact that they were both laughing at him didn't help the situation.

Kareem chuckled as Marquise took another shot to the head.

"So let me get this straight, fool," Kareem began. "You irritated because the kids are... being kids?"

"Not like that, man. You know what I mean," Marquise defended himself.

"No we don't, nigga, obviously, that's why he askin'," Blaze countered.

"What I'm sayin' is their toys are everywhere. They running, playing, and breaking shit all over the crib!" Marquise said before gulping down some beer.

"Nigga, that's what kids do! You do remember what that was like, right?" Kareem added with a laugh.

The mere mentioning of his childhood brought back unpleasant memories of his mother.

"I'm just not used to this shit, man. I didn't know shit was gone be this hard, you feel me?" Marquise asked.

Blaze sipped his beer before responding. "Look, you love Naomi, right?"

Marquise nodded his head in agreement. "Yeah, I love her and the kids, too."

"Well, then you gotta man up, fool! You can't be gettin' all mad and shit every time they get shit messy or break sumthin'. You a family man now and it ain't like it used to be. It's not just about you no more," Blaze reiterated.

Although Marquise knew what Blaze was saying was true, he was still frustrated to say the least.

"I feel what you sayin tho', Marq. What you and Naomi doing is different from anything you ever done. You sure you ready?" Kareem asked.

At that moment, Marquise really thought about what he was asking. Yes, he loved Naomi, Josie, and Christopher with everything in him. Were there somethings that he was going to have to get used to? Absolutely.

"A'ight, look, I was watching some parenting show the other day, right? And they were saying that you gotta use reverse psychology on the kids and shit. Like cleaning and stuff. Setting up a reward system... you know, shit like that," Blaze said.

Both Kareem and Marquise looked at each other before they both began to laugh.

"The fuck is so funny?" Blaze laughed.

"Nigga, what you doing watchin' parenting shows? You turning into Dr. Phil or some shit?" Kareem joked.

Marquise laughed at his boys. Even though it was funny to think about, he knew what Blaze was saying made sense. He just hoped he could sort through the bullshit.

"There's somethin' else," Marquise blurted out before he had the chance to think about what he was saying.

"What, fool?" Kareem questioned as they both listened intently.

"Rose been callin' me... she says she wanna see me. She wanna meet face to face," he admitted.

Kareem and Blaze remained silent. They knew all about Rose and what she did to their boy when he was a kid. They were beyond loyal to one another, so with that being said, they didn't care for Rose even if they didn't know her. Just the facts alone left a bad taste in their mouths when it came to her.

"So what you gone do?" Kareem asked.

"Don't know yet. A part of me wants to, but the other part of me hates her soul," he reiterated.

"I get it. Whatever you decide to do, we support you, bro. Fucked up how she wanna pop back into your life after all these years," Blaze added.

Marquise just nodded his head. He knew they felt the same way he did about the situation. It felt good to know that his boys had his back and understood him. As far as he was concerned, they were all the family he really needed.

CHAPTER 16

Naomi flipped through her magazine trying to take her mind off of all that was going wrong in her life at the moment. Although she originally thought that her and Marquise were good, she now felt different. That just didn't sit well with her at all. He'd been staying gone most of the day and not spending as much time with her and the kids as usual. She had the feeling that he was purposely staying away, but what she didn't understand was why?

Was it something she'd said? Had she unintentionally made him angry? She was clueless, while he ran the streets leaving her in the dark. She didn't understand how they'd gotten to this place within their relationship. They'd almost always been on the same page and talked about everything. Now she felt like Marq was switching up on her and she didn't like it one bit.

Sure, she knew he was dealing with his own stuff considering his mother decided to pop back into his life. But, that didn't mean that it was okay to take it out on her. Naomi grabbed her phone from the sofa next to her and decided to give him a call.

"Hello?" he answered.

"Hey, you. Just checkin' on you. Haven't really seen or talked to you all day," Naomi said while nervously chewing her bottom lip.

"Yeah, I know, I been busy. You know how this shit go," he reassured her.

"Well, we miss you. The kids have been asking for you and wondering where you are," she declared.

Marquise chuckled. Naomi could picture the grin he was sporting at that very moment. It made her smile to know that the mere thought of her children had put a smile on his face.

"I miss y'all, too. What my babies doing anyway?" he inquired.

"Well, Josie is in the tub and Chris is in his room drawing. He said he was making something for y—" she attempted to speak.

"Yeah, a'ight. Look, I gotta go, I'll holla at you in a min," he rudely interrupted her before disconnecting the call.

What the fuck was that shit about? she thought to herself.

Naomi called him back. She just knew it had to be an accident. There was no way in hell Marquise had hung up on her.

Naomi's mouth fell open when his voicemail came on after only one ring.

"This nigga got me fucked up!" Naomi yelled as she threw her phone on the couch beside her.

She was beyond pissed. How dare he hang up in her face and then send her to voicemail? She never would have thought that her man would disrespect her in such a way. As far as she was concerned, he could stay wherever he was and he didn't have to call her back at all. Naomi felt that Marquise had fucked up and there was no reason in the world that could make her understand why he did what he did.

***

Marquise nervously rubbed his hands together as he approached the park bench. He saw her sitting there looking in the opposite direction as if she were waiting for someone. All the while it was him that she was waiting for. Marquise literally felt sick to his stomach as he approached the bench. He wanted so bad to turn around and walk back to his car. He would never have to hear from her again if he wanted it to be that way. But his legs had a mind of their own.

So many thoughts were swarming through his head as she turned towards him. She squinted her eyes as she observed him. Then her eyes suddenly widened with a sense of recognition. Rose stood up as tears sprang to her eyes. She extended her arms for a hug. Initially, he struggled with the idea, but then decided to just go with it.

Marquise reciprocated the hug, returning her embrace.

"Marquise, my baby boy, it's so good to see you," she cried into his chest.

He remained silent as he allowed her to hold on to him. Rose was short with a dark caramel complexion. Although she'd put on a few pounds, being the curvy woman that she was, it only added to her beauty. Her long thick hair was pulled back into a ponytail at the nape of her neck.

When she released him, she stared up at him with tear-filled hazel eyes that were identical to his. "Sit with me," she said as she held his hand and took a seat on the bench.

Marquise did as he was asked and took a seat next to her. He clenched his fists in attempt to hide his true feelings. He was nervous, angry, sad, and elated at the same damn time. He didn't know what to say so he felt that he shouldn't say anything at all. Rose had asked for a chance to speak and he was going to allow her to do just that.

Sensing his apprehension, Rose began to speak.

"I know that I haven't been the best parent in the world. I know that I haven't been half of the woman that I should have to you boys. I tried my best though, and if you only knew all that I been through in my life, you would truly understand why I am the way I am."

Marquise glared at her. Was she fucking serious?

"I did the best with what I had and struggled like hell to keep a roof over our heads. But none of that was ever enough and the bills just kept piling up. We were almost homeless when I met Al. He gave me money for clothes, food, bills, and anything extra you boys may have wanted. For the first time in my life, I felt loved by a man. A man who I felt that I didn't deserve," she admitted as she stared off into space.

Marquise felt tears begin to sting his eyes as he bit down hard on his bottom lip. He was trying hard to hold his emotions inside.

"That night when he came to the house, he said he was tired of coming so far on that side of town to see me. That he wanted me to be closer to him, so that we could wake up next to each other and that we could get married. I told him that we couldn't just up and leave, because you and your brother were enrolled in school. I told him that it was a bad idea to think that you guys would be okay with leaving your friends and lives behind," Rose explained.

Marquise could feel heat rising from the tips of his toes to the top of his head. How could she sit here and make him relive this story as if it hadn't been his own? As if it hadn't hurt him enough to have to go through it initially.

"He said that you boys were almost men and could look after yourselves. He promised that he would pay all of the bills in the house and give you both a monthly allowance to have for yourselves. He lied to me for months!" Rose cried as tears poured from her eyes.

"How long?" Marquise asked.

"What?" Rose responded.

"How long did it take you to realize that he had left us for dead? How long did it take for you to realize that you hadn't checked on your kids and that you didn't know if they were dead or alive?" Marquise yelled.

Rose cried as she shook her head from guilt. She turned towards him to look him directly in the eyes.

It was then that he saw it. From the bottom of her neck to her temple was a long ugly scar. Marquise wasn't positive, but to him it appeared to be a burn that turned into a keloid.

Marquise stuck his hand underneath her chin and turned her face around so that he could get a full view. He carefully observed the wound before looking back into her eyes. Rose nodded her head as more tears poured from her eyes.

"Did your knight in shining armor do that to you?" he asked as his eyes began to burn.

"Yes. He did it when I found out that he'd been lying to me, I confronted him. He sliced me across the face with a letter opener and then poured a bottle of alcohol on my face," she admitted while looking down at her hands.

Marquise felt his heart skip a beat as more anger rose inside of him.

"I love you and your brother, Marq. I swear I did, even though I made bad decisions. After what happened to me, I was too ashamed and fell into deep depression. I felt like you both were better off without me," she yelled.

He looked at her and said, "Everything we got after you left, we struggled for. We had nothing and when my brother was killed, I was all alone! I had no one to turn to except the streets. While you were wallowing in self-pity, I was serving my first rock! I was a kid, Ma! A fuckin' kid who was forced to grow up too fast and made a lot of dumb mistakes because I didn't have nobody to show me the way!"

Rose reached out her hands to wipe away the tears that fell from Marquise's eyes. Tears that he hadn't realized had fallen. He pushed her hand away before beginning to speak again.

"I hurt a lot of people along the way. I made a lot of fucked up decisions, too, but not one time did I turn my back on nobody who'd been loyal to me, period! See, I learned a lot from you and I made somethin' of myself. I have brothers who love me and they are my real family. They been right by my side and got my back no matter what," he declared before wiping the tears from his face.

"I'm your family too, Marq, and I'm only trying to make this right!" Rose cried.

Marquise sighed. He could acknowledge her effort, but to him it was too little too late. She could save that shit for somebody who cared.

"Thank you for speakin' yo' peace. Now that we both got that shit off our chest, it's time to go back to reality. I have my life and you have whatever it is that you have. But, with that being said, our lives are still separate. I'm glad to see you doing okay and to know that you still alive, but I don't need none of this in my life right now," Marquise spoke as he stood up.

"Marq, please! Can I at least call or text you every now and then?" a defeated Rose begged.

He contemplated her question. He knew by agreeing, he would be potentially opening a door that there would be no going back through. If he allowed Rose to be a part of his life, that would mean that in time he would have to forgive her for all of her wrongdoings.

"Yeah, that's fine. But, I'm not promising you nuthin' so don't be blowin my shit up," he stated.

Rose smiled as she nodded her head in agreement. She knew that her son was trying and that's all she ever wanted.

"Take care of yourself, baby boy," she smiled as she turned to walk away in the opposite direction.

Marquise watched until she'd turned the corner and was completely out of sight. He too began walking. Marquise felt like a huge weight had been lifted off of his shoulders regardless of the outcome. For years he'd been contemplating what he'd say whenever he saw her again. Now that he finally had the chance, he could honestly say he felt better.

Marquise stood outside of his Ferrari for a moment. He then looked up to the sky and smiled to his deceased brother. He knew he'd be proud of him for making amends with their mother. Furthermore, he'd just be proud that his little brother had made it out alive.

CHAPTER 17

Tyree: *Naomi please it's been a few days. I need to see my kids.*

Tyree: *Please I know my kids miss me too.*

Tyree: *I know you don't love me no more, but my kids do.*

Naomi rolled her eyes as his last text came through. She glanced over at the kids who were sitting on the couch watching TV. She knew Tyree was right and she had to let them see him again eventually. To be honest, she was in need of a break and could use some time alone. She was having a hard time dealing with the issues within her relationship with Marquise at the moment. Naomi was beginning to have some serious doubts about her decision to move in with him.

Lately, Marquise had been moody and ignoring her. He barely answered her phone calls and sweet texts had become a thing of the past. Naomi was fed up and needed some air so that she could clear her head.

Naomi: *Ok, I'll bring them over in a few hours.*

Tyree: *Thank you.*

Tyree: *I still love you, Naomi.*

Naomi didn't bother to respond. She knew exactly what Tyree was trying to do and she wasn't falling for it, no matter how bad things had gotten. Despite it all, Marquise still had her heart. Naomi still remained head over hills in love with him and prayed that they got it together.

"Kids, we need to clean up so you can get ready. Your dad wants to spend some time with you today," Naomi announced.

"Yay!" Josie yelled.

"Okay, Mommy," Christopher responded.

Naomi noticed he wasn't too enthused about seeing his father. Josie skipped off down the hallway as Naomi approached her son to find out what was going through his head.

"Chris, you okay?" she questioned.

"Yeah, I'm okay," he responded.

"Why the long face? You're not happy about going to see your dad?" she asked.

"Yeah I am… it's just I been waiting for Marq to have time so that I can show him the game level I got on."

Naomi felt as if her heart had been torn in two. Her kids could obviously sense the change in Marquise just as she had, and it hurt her.

"I promise you'll get to show it to him tonight after he comes home. I'll make sure of it," Naomi declared.

Slowly, but surely, a smile spread across his face causing his eyes to light up. Just like that, all of his worries were gone and Chris was happy once again. Naomi watched as he, too, ran down to hallway to get ready for a visit with his father.

All the while leaving Naomi to her troubled thoughts.

***

Naomi waved goodbye to her kids as she made her way back to the condo she shared with Marquise. A sense of relief passed over her at the thought of taking a hot bubble bath and reading a good book while the kids were gone. Tyree had asked if the kids could spend the night, but ultimately she'd disagreed. She just didn't feel comfortable with that just yet with everything that had happened. For all she knew, Tyree was still fucking around with Erin and she didn't want that mess around her kids.

Naomi looked down at her phone to find a text coming through.

773-212-8784: *Naomi, please can we talk?*

773-212-8784: *I really just miss my best friend. I know I was wrong and I hurt you.*

773-212-8784: *Can we meet? I'm begging you, please.*

Naomi was so annoyed with Erin and her attempts. She had no clue why this girl was still trying to talk to her after what she'd done. Of course she realized that she couldn't ignore the elephant in the room forever, but she was perfectly fine with ignoring it for now. More or so often her mother's words resounded in her head.

"Sweetie, sometimes people are messed up. Their way of thinking and loving is just messed up. At the end of the day, there's nothing you can do to change that. But, when you forgive someone it's not for them, it's for you to release the burden of pain you carry around with you daily. Letting go of the pain is the only way to fully move on with your life. Besides, your cordial with Tyree, right? Well, then you can at least have a

conversation with Erin to let her know where you two stand. When you're ready, you'll know, trust me."

No matter how hard her mother tried to convince her that forgiving them was the way, she just wasn't in the forgiving mood. She hadn't forgiven Tyree for anything. All she wanted to do was be a good mom and by doing so that meant she had to co-parent with their no good dad. That was all to it for now.

Naomi stepped out of her car and made her way inside of the condo. She rode the elevator to their floor and hopped off. Once she stuck her key in the door and looked around, all she could do was smile. There was nothing. There was no one. Naomi poured herself a glass of wine and began to run herself some bath water. She lit candles and then stripped out of her clothes before sliding inside.

She moaned when the warm water and bubbles kissed her skin. Her body was tired and stiff. She was in much need of this me time and she was going to take full advantage of it. Naomi leaned her head back and closed her eyes. Before she knew it she'd dozed off.

She was awakened by the touch of fingers sliding across her collarbone. Naomi opened her eyes to find Marquise sitting at the edge of the tub with a sexy smile on his face.

"Yo' ass almost drowned in there," he laughed.

"Yeah right, nigga," she chuckled as he handed her a towel.

She stood up and wrapped the towel around her before grabbing a hold of his hand. Marquise helped her out of the tub, all the while ogling her body. No matter what was going on, Naomi always turned him on. She was his and he loved her. To him, everything about her was beautiful.

Marquise blew out the candles before following her into the bedroom.

"Uh-uh, I got that," he interrupted her just as she was about lotion up.

Naomi smiled as he removed the bottle from her hand and poured some inside of his palm. He then began to rub it on her shoulders while giving her a massage at the same time.

Moans filled the room as Naomi enjoyed the special attention she was getting from her man. This was the Marquise she knew and loved.

Her man had finally returned and she welcomed him back with open arms.

"If you keep rubbing on my back like that you gone get yourself in trouble," she teased.

"I love the kind of trouble you give, baby," Marquise whispered in her ear as he gently sucked on her earlobe.

"Good, because your pussy misses you and we're kid free," she clarified.

The most beautiful smirk graced his lips as he began to place sweet kisses on her collarbone.

"Kids staying all night?" he asked in between kisses.

"Of course not. I'm not ready for all of that after what he did," she stated in between moans.

Suddenly, he stopped kissing her and Naomi felt a cool breeze of air whisk past her. She looked over to find that Marquise had exited the room. Naomi quickly grabbed her silk robe and slid into it before following him into the living room.

"Marq? What is the problem?" she asked as he stood in front of her glaring with a look of disdain on his face.

"So you been takin' the kids by there to see that nigga even after we discussed this? You been sneakin' behind my damn back?" he yelled.

"What? Marq, I thought we talked about this already? Tyree is their father and is going to be a part of my life, regardless! You have to get used to that!" Naomi yelled.

"Yes, I said I would get used to it, but you never even gave me time to adjust. Damn Naomi, you don't ever consider how some shit gone make me feel before you do it! It's like you don't give a fuck about my opinion at all," he added.

Naomi's mouth hung open. He didn't say what she thought he said.

"You know what, Marq, I have had it with this shit. I am tired of walking on egg shells around here when it comes to your opinions. I am those kids' mother and it's my job to make the best decisions for them. You stay gone only to climb into bed at night and then leave before any of us wake up, and you expect me to respect some shit?" Naomi clarified.

Marquise began to speak but was cut off by Naomi. She was furious and had a huge weight to get off of her chest. Marq was going to hear what she had to say, because frankly she was sick of his shit.

"What in the hell do you want me to do, Marquise? Chase you? Nag? I mean, come on, give me a fuckin' break here! I am tired of crying and fighting with you over these kids seeing their dad. I am sick of your nonchalant attitude and frankly, I'm sick of you giving a fuck only when it hurts your pride! Meanwhile, Chris didn't want to leave the house without knowing if he was going to see you soon so that he can show you the game level he got to finally! He also made a drawing for the both of you! You are the one making things difficult right now... not me!" she cried as tears sprung from her eyes.

A frustrated Marquise glared at Naomi and said, "Naomi, stop tryna make this shit about them kids seein' they damn daddy! You already know why I have a problem with this shit, so don't play dumb! He don't deserve to wake up to they smiling faces every morning and make them breakfast! He don't deserve to know how they day went or who hurt they feelings at school! He let them down when he let you down! My problem is you don't realize what type of man you have in front of you and I'm tired of arguing with yo' ass too! So let me do us both a favor and leave you the fuck alone!"

Naomi cried as he stormed towards the front door.

"That's right, run away, Marq! That's all you know how to do lately!" she screamed as the door slammed shut.

Naomi fell to the floor and wept. She was so tired of the drama. All she wanted to do was to be happy. Why couldn't Marq understand that? For the life of her she just couldn't understand why he continued to fight her so hard on the issue.

Ding!

Naomi sighed as she got up from the floor and made it to her phone which lay on her bed. She unlocked her screen to find a text message.

Tyree: *I miss this... us being a family. I want my family back.*

Tyree: *I know you miss this, too. I'm so sorry I fucked it up. But let's just make things right again, baby.*

CHAPTER 18

Blaze: *Spoke to Sergio.*

Kareem: *So he know 'bout you not takin' the offer now?*

Blaze: *Yeah, he does.*

Marquise: *A'ight.*

Marquise: *It's for the best though. Anika don't want you doin' that and you gotta respect her wishes.*

Blaze: *Yup.*

Kareem: *You heard from her yet?*

Blaze: *Nah.*

Blaze: *You heard from Sadie?*

Kareem: *Nah.*

Blaze: *You know they togetha right?*

Kareem: *How you know?*

Blaze: *Anika ain't got no family but her. They definitely togetha.*

Kareem: *Guess we just gotta keep givin' them space.*

Blaze: *Yeah... Space.*

Marquise: *See y'all niggas in a few hours?*

Blaze: *Bet.*

Kareem: *Yeah man. See y'all soon.*

It had only been fifteen minutes after texting his boys and working on some renovations for his night club that Marquise received a call from Kareem, informing him of the trouble at their main warehouse. It was being burnt down.

Marquise could only quickly get himself together and head straight to meet up with his boys, extremely pissed off at the current situation. And he knew exactly who was behind it all.

***

"Yeah, so the attorney has the documents with all the shit that could put that fool away for a very long time," Marquise stated firmly.

"With everything he's done, I hope he never comes out, and drops the soap," Kareem announced before turning to Blaze who had been awfully silent during the conversation. "Blaze, you good, nigga?"

Blaze looked up at 'Reem only to nod. "Yeah, I'm good."

"I know how much the warehouse meant to you," Marquise said. "How much it meant to us all. Especially because of how hard we worked on making it solid and filled with all the stock that helped us become better ova the years."

Marquise still couldn't believe it. Their main warehouse had been burnt to ashes. There was absolutely nothing left and now they were left without a main house for their squad.

"Yeah, and we definitely had a lot of good memories ova there," Kareem stated coolly. "I'ma miss it."

"We got the others though," Marquise reminded the boys. "They not as big, but we could get some renovations done or some shit."

Blaze simply nodded at his boys, but decided to stay silent. Marquise figured his boy was just taking it all in and getting used to their predicament.

"Jamal's the brains behind The Lyons' whole operation," Marquise explained. "Without him, they're just regular ass niggas, with no proper expertise on the streets and what to do against us. Notice how mediocre those niggas were when Jamal wasn't 'round?"

"Oh, yeah, I remember. They were just movin' small weight 'round on the streets," Kareem voiced. "Then that first attack on our boy happened. And after that, shit went left from there."

"That's 'cause they had Jamal helpin' them," Blaze suddenly intervened. "We really just gon' have to take him down and they'll be defenseless without him. If he's the brains behind their own operation, they gon' be nothin' without him."

"Exactly," Kareem responded. "We just gotta focus on bringin' him down."

"Why do you think he agreed to start workin' wit' them in the first place?" Marq queried.

"Money," Blaze suggested. "Greed… Anika."

Jamal had actually been Anika's old boss before she got into a serious relationship with Blaze. Blaze knew that Jamal must have realized that Anika was seeing Blaze, and working with Leek would have been the perfect opportunity to get revenge on Blaze.

"Well now they all gon' regret comin' for us from the very start," Kareem confidently announced. "Cause when we done with them, they gon' wish they had neva been born."

"Believe that," Marquise concluded.

"Yup," Blaze agreed. "We definitely gon' finish them once and for all."

"And after we finish them, we can start workin' on how y'all gon' get yo' chicks back," Marquise declared. He knew how upset and depressed his boys were without their girls.

"I'm tired of givin' Sadie space," Kareem said with a groan. "I miss her crazy ass."

"Lord knows I miss Anika," Blaze voiced. "All this space shit is depressin'. I'on wanna do it no more."

"Me neither," Kareem agreed.

"So what'chu wanna do, niggas?" Marquise questioned them both curiously.

They both kept silent before Blaze came to a conclusion.

"I'ma go get her back today."

Kareem decided to follow suit. "Same here, nigga. I'm done wit' this whole break shit. She loves me, I love her, we just gotta fix this shit."

"So y'all just gon' leave and head to Sadie's?"

Kareem and Blaze both nodded in agreement before getting out their seats, saying their goodbyes to Marq then leaving.

Marquise wished shit could be as simple with him and Naomi, but it wasn't. Things had been pretty rocky between them and unfortunately, that's just the way things were.

Was it his fault that he felt some type of way towards Tyree after all that he had done to Naomi? Was it his fault that he hated the guy and didn't want Naomi to have anything to do with him ever again?

Naomi just didn't seem to understand that Marquise wasn't happy about what she was doing. Going to see Tyree with the kids without discussing it with him first, was one of the things that had really irritated Marq. He planned to marry her one day, but how could he marry a woman that didn't even discuss things with him and just did things to the beat of her own drum?

He couldn't do that. He liked to be the man and he liked to have control, that's just the way he was. And Naomi knew this about him from the start, so why she was acting up now had him very confused.

And the kids... Oh the kids!

Marquise loved them like they were his own. They meant so much to him and he wanted to be a much better father than Tyree ever could. It didn't matter that Chris and Josie weren't actually his, he loved them like they were. But as much as he loved them, he wasn't used to them living with him 24/7, being around his space, and everything. He had never lived with kids before, so doing it now was strange. He couldn't help but become angry when something was broken, or when the kids became quite annoying. He just wasn't used to them living in his environment 24/7.

But everyone had to learn how to adjust to new things somehow, right?

***

Marquise slowly turned his key in his lock before pushing through his door.

He was eager to see Naomi. He really wanted to talk to her, apologize for his behavior towards her yesterday, and straighten things out with her. They needed to get to a clear understanding of how things were going to work in their relationship and what they needed to do together as a couple.

"Naomi!" Marquise called out to her as he walked through his apartment. "Baby, where you..."

Marquise's words suddenly trailed off when he entered his bedroom and clocked Naomi standing at the edge of the bed.

She didn't bother looking at him once he came in, she only continued to pack her clothes one by one into her purple suitcase.

"Naomi, what you doin'?"

She wasn't here to talk, explain, or argue. She was just here to get her things and bounce. She had already packed the kids' things up and placed them into her car. All that was left to do was pack her things up.

She was done.

"Naomi, I asked you a question," he snapped.

Even though she could feel his hard glare on her and hear the growing frustration in his voice, she didn't care. She wasn't about to let him intimidate her. She was done.

Naomi continued to pack the last remaining items into her suitcase and once everything was packed, she zipped her suitcase and was ready to leave.

She was too afraid to look Marquise in the eye, so all she did was drag her suitcase along behind her and walk towards the door. Only issue was as soon as she got to the door, Marquise blocked her path and immediately kicked her suitcase down before pulling her by her arms.

"I said what the fuck are you doin', Naomi?!" he yelled, roughly shaking her by the arms. "Why are you walking out of here with a suitcase in your hands?"

"I'm done, Marquise," she quietly announced.

Marquise couldn't believe it. He knew it had to be a dream. The more he looked into her eyes, the more he saw nothing but disappointment. Disappointment that he just didn't understand.

"What do you mean you done?"

"I'm done with this relationship, Marquise."

"No, you fucking ain't!" he fumed, leaning in closer to her. "You ain't done with nothing!"

"Yes I am," she pushed boldly. "I'm no longer doing this, Marquise. I'm no longer doing the arguments, the mood swings. I'm taking my kids and I'm doing what you want me to do. I'm leaving you alone."

Marquise couldn't believe what she was saying right now. He couldn't believe the words coming out of her lips right now. Was she serious? She was trying to leave him? After all the shit they had been through to get back together. After all he had done for her. All the time he had invested in her.

"Are you dumb?" he rudely queried. "You're not leavin' me alone! You're not taking the kids anywhere either. You're staying with me."

"Clearly you're not listening to what I'm saying properly, Marquise," Naomi voiced. "I'm not staying with a man that I'm no longer sure about. A man that I don't even know loves me the way I lo—"

"You know damn well how much I love you, Naomi," Marquise cut her off. "Don't play with me, this is some absolute bullshit if you think I'm letting you le—"

"No, this isn't some absolute bullshit, Marq! This is nothing, but facts right now." Naomi pushed Marquise away from her and managed to escape his grip. "I didn't decide to leave Ty to be treated like shit by you. I didn't decide to leave Ty to be in a relationship dominated mainly by you. I didn't decide to leave Ty to be in a relationship with a man who isn't grown enough to handle my kids! I didn't! And I won't stand for it now at all," Naomi cried, feeling her eyes beginning to burn. "I'm done, Marq. I'm leaving and that's that. You're not going to change my mind about the situation, so please just let me go."

Marquise could only feel his anger rapidly building as Naomi spoke to him. First, he didn't appreciate the way she was talking to him at all and secondly, he knew all she was saying was just bloody excuses. She just wanted to leave him, because she was scared. She was a scared little girl, not grown enough to handle a thug like him.

"You know what, Naomi, if you really wanna leave then you can go ahead and do that shit. I ain't gonna stop you, you know why? Because you're no longer worth the chase. 'Cause that's what your stupid ass wants right? For me to chase you! That's all you've ever wanted. You knew who I was the second you started fucking with me, you knew I didn't play no games, and you definitely knew that all I ever wanted to do was make you happy. My behavior for the last few days have mostly been because of you and your selfish nature. You taking the kids to see Tyree without me knowing, was out of order! And you knew it too, which is why you didn't tell me straight away."

"They're my kids, Marquise, not yours! I can do whatever the hell I want with them. They depend on me, not you," she spat. "I'm not going to stand here and continue to argue with you. I'm done and that's that."

"Alright, go then! See if I care, I don't need you, Naomi. Go!"

Naomi quickly picked up her suitcase that Marquise had kicked over, and pulled up its silver handle to hold. It was time for her to set out with what she had originally planned to do. Leave him. He wanted her gone then that was fine by her.

Just as Naomi managed to push past Marquise and pull her suitcase behind her, he decided to speak up.

"So you really gonna go after all the shit we've been through, Naomi?"

Naomi sighed softly at his words. One minute he wanted her gone, the next minute he wanted her to stay. His crazy nature was really coming out right now.

"You think it's okay to leave me after everything we've built over the past couple months together? All we've talked about doing together? Are you fuckin' serious right now?"

"I am serious!" Naomi exclaimed, turning back round to face him. "I am dead ass serious right now. If I hadn't met you, my family would be absolutely fine. I wouldn't have neglected my husband and fallen for you. Everything would have been absolutely fine. I still would have my family and you wouldn't have me! You wouldn't have my heart the way you've had it these past couple months."

"Had it?" Marquise looked at her with a confused facial expression as a tiny tear fell out his left eye. "You sayin' you don't love me anymore? Is that what you sayin' right now?"

"I... I'm just done, Marquise," Naomi quietly answered, no longer in the mood to shout at him especially now that tears were leaving his eyes. Her eyes only continued to burn the more she watched his. She knew that if she didn't leave now, she wasn't going to be able to stop the incoming water works. "It was fun while we started, but we both know you're not ready for this. For my kids or for a real serious relationship. I'm just going to get things back to how they used to be, because that's what's best for my kids. And I only want what's best for my kids... I'm sorry." Naomi quickly pulled on her suitcase handle before dragging it on behind her.

"No!" Marquise furiously yelled, pulling Naomi's suitcase back.

"Marquise, leave me alone, please! I need to g-"

"No! I'm not letting you leave me. You know how much I love you, Naomi, and I know how much you love me, too! You can't be considering going back to that nigga and leavin' me with nothing. I'm not letting you go... I can't... I can't, Naomi."

Naomi felt her heart breaking into a million pieces the more she stared into Marquise's teary hazel eyes. Tears were only falling faster and faster down his eyes making Naomi emotional. She wished she could tell him that she wasn't going anywhere. That she was never going to leave him like this, but unfortunately she wasn't. She had to do what she thought was best for her kids and that was that.

"Marquise, let me go," Naomi ordered, grabbing onto her suitcase handle and trying to move it out of Marquise's tight grip.

"No, you ain't goin', Naomi."

"Yes I am," she affirmed. "This is over and the sooner you realize that, the easier this will be. We're over, Marquise, and you're not changing my mind."

All Marquise could do was remain frozen as Naomi pushed his hands off her suitcase and continued to drag it along behind her. He didn't even bother trying to stop her anymore once she was out the door and heading to his living room. And once he heard his front door open and quickly shut, the tears didn't stop flowing.

He stepped closer to his open door and immediately kicked it hard, feeling a vast amount of anger stir within him.

He couldn't believe for one second that she had actually had the confidence to walk out of his life. He thought that she was going to stay with him forever. He wanted her to stay with him forever.

But now she was gone and Marquise could only crouch down to the floor with sadness and cry painfully.

Why the fuck would she leave him knowing how much he loved her? How was he supposed to live without her?

CHAPTER 19

It had only been a day without her and the kids and Marquise still couldn't function properly without them.

Things didn't feel the same without them here and it certainly didn't look the same either. He missed the liveliness that the kids had brought to his crib, he missed seeing Naomi in the kitchen whipping up a meal for them all. He just missed them.

He considered ringing Naomi and begging for her to come back, but his pride wouldn't allow him to at all. She was the one that had left him, so there was no point of forcing her to do something she clearly didn't want to do anymore.

Marquise wanted to call up his boys and ask them for some advice, but he wasn't in the mood to pour out all his problems to them, especially when he knew that they had just gotten their problems sorted with their girls. They were no longer fighting and all back together.

But now Marquise was the one having problems with his girl.

He decided on calling Rose. He figured that if anyone would be willing to listen to the bullshit going on in his life right now, it would be her.

"Marquise?"

"Yeah, it's me…"

"I'm so happy you called. What's up son? You sound… down."

"I'm just going through some shit right now, could use someone to talk to."

"I'm all ears."

***

While the kids played happily outside, Naomi struggled to keep her emotions in line. She couldn't stop thinking about Marquise and what had become of their relationship in the last twenty-four hours. She couldn't believe that they were over and it didn't matter how many times she tried to convince herself that this was all for the best, she couldn't.

She really just prayed that she was doing the right thing and that things would be good for the sake of her family.

"Baby, you good?"

Naomi gasped quietly at the sudden touch of Tyree's hands on her waist.

"Yeah," she sheepishly replied, trying to get used to his touch on her body. She wished it was Marquise's though.

"You've made the right decision," he commented.

"What do you mean?" Naomi queried, keeping her eyes on Chris and Josie who were racing each other across the garden.

"Leaving that gangster. He was never going to treat you as well as I treated you."

All Naomi could do was bite her tongue and remain silent. She didn't want to start an argument with Tyree right now at all.

"He doesn't know you as well as I do, Naomi. He doesn't love you as well as I do and he certainly doesn't know how to make you feel as good as I do."

Naomi could hear herself chuckling in her head at Tyree's foolish words. He was just trying to make himself feel better and big up his ego. If Naomi wasn't so determined on getting her family back together right now, she wouldn't have hesitated in telling Tyree the truth about how Marq really made her feel.

"Why don't you come upstairs with me, Naomi, and let me remind you of just how good I can make you feel?"

"No," Naomi sternly responded, immediately pulling herself out of Tyree's arms.

"Why not, Naomi? If we're going to make this work, you need to listen to me, and I'm telling you I want to make you feel good right now."

"No," Naomi reiterated. "I need to go out somewhere." Naomi knew for a fact that even though she was getting back with Ty, he was never touching her ever again. Those days were long gone.

"To see my mom."

"Oh... Tell her I said hi," Tyree answered in a more understanding tone.

Naomi simply nodded before walking out into the garden to give her children a kiss goodbye. She was definitely no longer in the mood to be in the presence of Tyree. She just had to keep on reminding herself why she was doing this.

It's for the kids Naomi... Only for the kids.

***

"Alright, I agreed to meet up with you, Erin, so you could have the opportunity to explain whatever the hell you want to explain so bad."

So she had lied to Tyree about who she was going to meet up with, but so what?

Erin had been desperately calling up her phone for the past couple of weeks, so Naomi decided to take her out of misery and let her speak her mind.

Did this mean that Naomi was going to forgive her again and that they were going to be back singing kumbaya again?

Hell no.

But Naomi was willing to be an awfully good listener to Erin today and let her get what she wanted off her chest. That was it.

"Thank you for agreeing to meet up with me, Naomi," Erin said with a small smile. "I've missed you. You look good."

"I know I do," Naomi rudely stated. "Say what you need to say and be fast with it. I need to get back home to my kids and their father."

"Their father?"

"Don't act stupid, Erin," Naomi impatiently snapped. "You know exactly who I'm talking about."

"You're back with him?" Erin asked in a tone filled with nothing but surprise.

"And so what if I am?"

"I'm confused, you left Marq?"

"What's it to you, Erin? Look, just say what you need to say already."

"I slept with Tyree again," Erin blurted out.

"What?"

"I said... I slept with Tyree again," Erin repeated. "After you found out about us, we messed around again, a couple times. I know you didn't know and I figured you wouldn't really care, but now you've left Marquise to be with Tyree again, I'm just truly confused."

Naomi couldn't even speak.

She felt so much fury within her that she couldn't even keep still in her seat. She could feel her foot constantly tapping, her hips shuffling around slightly.

Erin and Tyree had been messing around again? Even after she had found out all they had been up to?

"I'm so sorry for everything, Naomi," Erin apologized. "All I ever wanted to do was make you happy. We've been best friends for years and you've always been there for me, I just wanted to be there for you."

This bitch.

Naomi couldn't even speak! Only regret began to overcome her once she had realized what she had done. Breaking up with Marquise was a mistake. Why had she done that shit?

Yes, they had been having problems in their relationship, but what couple didn't? He was the only man that had ever treated her like a Queen. He would never have slept with Erin the way Tyree had so freely.

And Erin, well she was just one stupid human being who Naomi knew for sure that she didn't want in her life anymore. There was no way she was going to allow Erin back into her life after the betrayal she had committed. She really believed in her sick little mind that sleeping with Tyree was going to be the best thing to do for Naomi?

How had that helped with anything? Tyree had only begun to neglect the kids and only turned more mean-spirited, drank more alcohol, and and was just become the worst person to be around 24/7.

So how the hell had Erin helped her situation in any shape or form?

"And I really hope you can find it in your heart to forgive me enough so we can be back to how we used to be."

As far as Naomi was concerned, she was officially done.

"Are you done?"

Done with Erin Jones and completely, utterly, undoubtedly done with Tyree Evans.

"Yeah, I guess I am... Naomi! Where are you going?"

Naomi stopped walking away from the table where Erin sat and decided to finish things once and for all.

"I've heard all the rubbish you had to say, Erin, and quite frankly, I really do not care. You so clearly want Tyree for yourself so you can have him all for yourself now, bitch. The both of you are now officially dead to me. I no longer want anything to do with you, so stop calling me... Matter fact, don't worry, call me all you'll like, we'll see if you actually get through this time." Naomi knew that the best thing to do to ensure Erin really got the message was to make sure she changed her number. That way Erin would no longer be able to bug her constantly.

"Please, Nao—"

"Stop it, Erin! I didn't come here to tell you that I forgive you. I didn't even come here to hear what bull you had to say. I just came to let you know that our friendship is dead and you need to move on."

Erin kept silent and only started to cry, leaving Naomi satisfied with the outcome. She just hoped and prayed that Erin finally got the message.

Their friendship was dead.

CHAPTER 20

"Kids, go get in the car, I'll be out in a second."

"Mom, where are we going?" Josie innocently asked.

"I'll answer your questions later, just please go get in the car."

Thank God Naomi hadn't decided to start unpacking straight away when they had arrived back home with Tyree. All the kids' things were still in their suitcases and so were hers. Their cases were already in the car. All that was left for her to do was get her cases into the trunk of her car and drive far, far, far away from here.

Deciding to try and "fix" things with Tyree for the sake of the kids was a huge mistake. A mistake Naomi definitely wasn't about to make again.

"And where do you think you're going?"

Naomi froze at the top of the stairs due to the deep voice she could hear come from behind her.

"I asked you a question, Naomi."

Naomi decided that the best thing to do would be to pay Tyree no mind and just to make it out the door. All she needed to do was make it out the door.

But the second she tried to run downstairs, a hand grabbed hold of her ponytail and instantly pulled her back into the main bedroom.

"Agh! Tyree, let me fucking go!"

"Where the hell do you think you're runnin' off to, bitch?"

Tyree had pulled her into their bedroom and pushed her to their shared bed. Now she was trapped, with nowhere to escape.

"I'm leaving you for good this time. I know you messed around with Erin again, so I'm going to leave you to it. I want a divorce, Tyree."

"Over my dead body!" he shouted. "You think I'm letting you leave me again? And taking my kids with you? So you can run back to that nigga? Girl, you must have lost your damn mind."

Naomi got up from the bed, stood on her feet in front of a frustrated, angry Tyree and only looked him dead in the eye.

"We are finished, Tyree, I'm not going to tell you this again."

"You're going to throw away our marriage for that stupid thug? That thug that doesn't really give a fuck about you? He's only usi—"

Slap! Slap! Slap!

Naomi couldn't control herself after the first slap. She was tired of hearing Tyree so freely insult Marquise, and after he had pulled her so aggressively into their bedroom, a slap was long overdue.

"Ow! Na—"

Slap! Slap! Slap!

Naomi only continued to slap him, adding a few punches here and there, too. All the anger she had kept deep inside her because of him, she decided to let out.

She didn't care that she was hurting him because that's exactly what her intentions were. And when he attempted to start fighting her back, Naomi only fought back harder. Every hit was inflicted in the hopes of him feeling as much pain as she did in her heart for leaving Marquise. A pain that she had caused for absolutely no reason. All he ever wanted to do was make her feel happy and she had suddenly out of the blue broken his heart. Again.

"Naomi, stop! Pl—"

"No! I'm not! You don't tell... me what... the fuck to do!"

It was only about a few minutes into attacking Tyree that Naomi felt a sharp pain the pit of her stomach.

She decided to stop attacking him and use this chance to get the hell out of this house.

Naomi ran out of the bedroom, grabbing her suitcase and immediately ran down the carpeted stairs.

It was only when she made it outside the house that she suddenly dropped her purple suitcase and bent over as a whole leap of vomit left her mouth.

She didn't understand why she was vomiting now all of a sudden. She only ever vomited when she was...

Pregnant.

No... She couldn't be?

Five minutes later, Naomi had gotten herself together and was now sitting in her driver's seat with the kids sitting behind.

"Mom, are you okay?" Chris questioned her curiously.

All Naomi could do was nod and start the car engine. She was going to drop the kids with her parents so she could clear her head.

The more she began to ponder over her current predicament, the more she was beginning to believe that she was pregnant.

When was the last time she had her period? She had definitely missed more than six weeks of her last menstrual. Also, her breasts had become quite tender and swollen over the past couple weeks, but she thought nothing of it. She had been urinating much more often than normal and found herself feeling tired at the strangest times.

The faster she drove to her parents' home, the more she continued to contemplate the situation.

She was pregnant with Marquise's child.

***

Marquise sighed deeply as he reminisced on all that had gone down in just a matter of eight months. Blaze had met Anika, Kareem and Sadie had finally hooked up, and he had met Naomi. He knew how much he loved Naomi and wanted to spend the rest of his life with her. He just wished that she hadn't broken up with him and run off back to her husband who didn't even respect her enough. He clearly hadn't respected Naomi when he went to go fuck around with her best friend. What kind of a man did that?

Marquise knew how much he wanted Naomi back. He had talked well enough with his mother over the phone to know that he wanted to spend the rest of his entire life with her. His mother advised him to just giving Naomi some space. She would soon come back to her senses and realize how much she loved him.

In just a matter of eight months, The Lyons had foolishly tried to come for the Knight Nation and only continued to fail. Yeah, they had attacked their turfs a few times, managed to take Anika, and blown up their entire warehouse, but those were all petty, low blows. Compared to what the Knight Nation could really do, The Lyons' acts so far had all been child's play.

If it wasn't for Blaze's promise to Anika about not killing Jamal, then Marquise was sure that Blaze wouldn't have hesitated in spending an entire day hunting him down and murdering him. But Marquise understood that Blaze's promise to Anika was more important to him than just getting revenge. Shit was changing because of who they were all in love with, and Marq knew that things were only changing for the good.

Just as Marquise decided to leave the new main warehouse, he heard the sudden bang of metal against the entrance door downstairs.

He knew he was the only one there, so if trouble was around, he would have to be strong enough to defend himself.

He immediately lifted the back of his red shirt, only to reach for the blue .9mm hiding in the waistband of his black jeans.

Once the metal banging had stopped, Marquise kept still and listened carefully for the sound of movement, coming up the stairs to the second floor where he was. But he seemed to hear none.

Slowly, he crept out the room he was in. Quickly, he looked left and right down the wooden corridors, each attached with a long staircase leading downstairs. It was when he stepped completely out the room that the first bullet came flying.

Bang!

Marquise quickly ducked, trying to take cover, but also wanting to see the person who was starting trouble with him tonight. But he could already sense it was Leek or one of those other fools in their squad. It couldn't be Jamal though. One thing the boys had noticed about Jamal was that he never liked doing dirty work himself, he preferred someone doing it for him.

Bang! Bang! Bang!

Marquise couldn't take it anymore. He needed to know because if it ended up being Leek, then he wouldn't hesitate in sending a single bullet through his head.

Marquise jumped up, gun in hand and looked over the balcony to see who was on the ground floor shooting bullets up at him.

The minute his eyes locked onto Leek's determined ones, Marquise didn't hesitate in cocking his gun back and gunning straight for him.

If he had to be the one to end this fool tonight, then so be it.

Bang! Bang! Bang!

Shots began to fly over both of their heads and Marquise continued to fire his ammo, focused on finishing this guy once and for all.

It was only a few quick seconds later when Marquise sent one final shot that managed to hit Leek straight in the head.

One shot, one kill, and Leek had collapsed straight to the floor.

Marquise always knew that one day all those shooting range lessons that Blaze had set up for him and Kareem all those years back, were always going to come in handy.

Just when Marquise wanted to jump with joy that he had finally gotten rid of Leek, he felt a sharp pain in his left leg and he looked down with fear only to see that he had been hit.

"Shit," he cursed.

The pain was now suddenly hitting him hard and blood was gushing out of his leg quite quickly. All he could do was slowly limp back into the office he was in before and reach for his phone.

There was only one person who he really wanted to speak to right now. He just prayed she picked up his call.

CHAPTER 21

Naomi drove around aimlessly as the thought about all that happened. She felt so stupid and most of all her heart ached. She'd went back to Tyree foolishly believing that she was making the best decision for her kids. In doing so, she'd pushed away the only man who had ever truly loved her. The one man who despite their differences, remained loyal and by her side no matter what transpired between them. She allowed her tears to flow freely from her eyes.

When she thought back to all the good times they shared within their relationship, she realized they truly outweighed the bad. Marquise was a solid, loving, devoted, and caring man. Did he have flaws? Yes, but hell, who didn't? As far as she was concerned, she'd take those flaws over any other man's any day.

Naomi sped towards the condo they shared in hopes of catching Marquise so that she could speak with him. So that she could tell him how foolish she'd been to walk out on him when all he wanted was what was best for both her and her kids. She desperately wanted to talk and clear the air so that they could move past all of the bullshit and drama. All she wanted to do was tell him how much she loved him and make things right.

Over and over in her mind, she replayed the very last moment she looked into his eyes. The moment she saw a tear fall because of the pain that she had caused. The way she crushed him with mere words that at the time she thought were best to say. When Marquise questioned the love she had for him, she allowed him to believe that she no longer loved him. Naomi did that simply because she knew that she wasn't strong enough to leave him on her own.

Naomi wiped away the tears from her face as she continued to drive. All the while, all she could do was pray that he was home and missed her as badly as she missed him. She prayed for his forgiveness.

Naomi glanced over at her passenger side seat to find her phone lighting up from a call that she was receiving. She sniffled as she quickly grabbed it and glared at the caller I.D. while trying to watch the road at the same time. Naomi gasped when she recognized the name on her screen. Marquise was calling and she had to pull herself together before answering. She exhaled before she did to prepare herself for whatever it was he had to say.

"Hello?" Naomi answered.

"Nao?" an out of breath Marq attempted to speak.

Naomi sat up in her seat as she placed him on speaker. Her gut told her something was wrong. Very wrong.

"Marq? Yes, baby, I'm here. What's wrong?" she questioned.

Nothing but heavy breathing filled her ears as she waited for him to speak. She could hear movement, but still no words left his lips.

"Marquise, what's going on? Talk to me!" a frantic Naomi panicked.

"Nao, I'm hit!" he confessed.

Naomi felt her stomach drop. Had she heard right? Had he said what she thought he said?

"Oh my God!"

"Naomi, I love you. All I can think about is how we argued and the way you left. Baby, I'm so sorry for everything I said. For everything I did wrong."

Naomi cried as his words touched her heart.

"I'm sorry too, baby. I didn't mean it, I swear. I love you, too."

"I love the kids and I want to be a family. I know I been trippin' lately. I fucked shit up between us cus' I was keepin' shit bottled up inside instead of talkin to you."

"It's okay, Marq. I know you love us. Where are you?"

"You my everything, Nao. I can't be without you, baby. I need you and the kids in my life. I'm not whole without y'all."

The realization hit her hard. Marquise was telling her his true feelings, because he didn't believe that he was going to make it. He was righting his wrongs because in his heart, he believed that he wasn't going to ever see her again.

"Marquise Lewis, tell me where you are!" she cried as tears streamed from her eyes.

"I'm at our warehouse," he declared.

"Where is it? I can help you, I just need to know how to get there!" she frantically questioned.

Marquise rattled off his whereabouts as Naomi busted a U-turn in the middle of the street. She recognized the location, because it was close to her favorite wine shop. A shop she only knew about because he had introduced her to it.

"Baby, I'm on my way, okay? Just stay with me, baby, please?" she pleaded.

Marquise continued to breath heavily on the line. Naomi felt as if her heart was going to burst through her chest as she drove through every stop sign and red light along the way. All the while praying that she got to him in time. She just had to because if she didn't she would never forgive herself.

"Marquise, you there?"

"Yeah... I'm here. Fuck!"

"Baby, you still with me?"

"I'm here. I'm startin' to get dizzy. I'm losin' too much blood," he confessed.

God please, if you save him for me I promise to be here for him from this point on. No more running. I promise God, please just save him for me. Do this one favor for me.

"Marquise, listen to me, okay?" Naomi said as she turned a corner damn near on two wheels heading straight for the warehouse.

"Baby, I need you. We need you. It's not just about us anymore and I can't live without you either. I love you with everything in me and I can't let you die on me. Marq, you gonna get through this okay? You gotta get through this because you gonna be a father!"

Naomi nervously listened as she heard a gasp come through the line just as she pulled up at the warehouse. She put the car in park, and hopped out with the engine still running. She ran to the front door to find a steel rod lodged between the handles on the door. She pushed and pulled as hard as she could, but the rod didn't budge.

"Marquise, I can't get in the front door! Is there another way inside?" she desperately asked.

"Ah! Shit!" he cried.

"Baby, tell me how to get in!"

"There's a door on the left side of the building."

Naomi took off in that direction, not before trippin' over a solid object on the ground in front of her. She hit the ground hard, knocking the wind out of her. She looked over to see what she tripped over to find a pair of feet. Her gazed traveled up to find the dead body of a man with a hole in his head paired with cold dead eyes staring up into the night's sky.

A scream tore through her as she peddled backwards until her back hit the wall. His lifeless body lay there in a pool of blood and a shocked Naomi sat there. She was quickly snapped back into reality when she heard Marquise's voice yelling from inside the warehouse.

"Naomi! Naomi!"

"I'm okay, bae. I'm coming!"

She got up off her ass and took off running in the direction of the side door, this time making sure she payed close attention to where she was going just in case there was another dead body lying around somewhere. She reached the side door finding an old tire up against the door handle. Using all her strength, she pushed it to the side before swinging the door open and running inside.

"Marq?" she yelled while allowing her eyes to adjust to the darkness.

"I'm up here!"

Naomi searched the darkness until she found a set of old wooden stairs and climbed them two at a time. Her heart was beating a mile a minute as she ran down the long stretch of hallway, desperately searching for her man. He just had to be okay. She was going to make sure that he was if it were the last thing she ever did.

Then in an instant, she reached the very last room on the right and laid eyes on him. There he sat with his back up against the wall, with his blue .9mm still firmly in his grip. He was sitting in a pool of his own blood. Naomi ran to his side, stopping only to remove his shirt from his body.

"Where is the blood coming from, baby? Is it here?" she asked.

When Marquise nodded yes, she proceeded to wrap the shirt around his bullet wound before tying it tightly.

"Ah! Shit!" he screamed.

Naomi kissed his cheek and lips in an attempt to suppress the pain. She knew it wasn't much, but all she wanted him to feel was that she was here for him.

"Baby, I need you to stand up so I can get you to a hospital. Can you do that?"

"Yeah," he declared between labored breaths.

Naomi used all of her strength to help Marquise get to his feet while leaning on her for support. She carefully guided him down the hallway, down the stairs, and then out of the door. As soon as she approached the car, she opened the back door and carefully helped him lay on the back seat. After closing the door behind him, she tore off into the darkness towards the nearest hospital.

"Godammit!" Marquise yelled out in agony.

"I know, baby, we almost there. I'll get us there, I promise," she said while looking through her rear view mirror and attempting to drive at the same time.

Naomi could barely see as the tears stung her eyes. She was trying so hard to be strong, but to see her man hurting the way he was killed her inside. Marquise was always so strong and the one to be there for her in her time of need. Now it was her turn to be strong for him. Naomi was determined to save his life.

Naomi glanced through her mirror again to see his eyes slowly closing as if he were about to fall asleep.

"Marq! Wake up, baby, stay with me! We're almost there!" she cried.

Marquise's eyes snapped back open as he fought to stay awake.

"God, please!"

"I love you, Nao," he declared before his eyes closed completely.

"Marquise! Marquise!" a frantic Naomi yelled as she pulled into the emergency room entrance. She ran to the front doors of the hospital, screaming for help before making her way back to the car.

"Marq, please wake up! Marquise, please!" she cried as medical staff filed out to assist her.

"Ma'am, we need you to step back," someone ordered.

Naomi continued to cry as she stepped back to allow them to do their job.

"Please save him," she begged.

CHAPTER 22

Marquise could faintly hear noise around him. The sound of beeping and of whispering filled the room. His eyes were heavy. They felt as if weights were holding them down. He tried to open his eyes, but failed miserably. He tried to move his arms. They too felt heavy. He moved his head to the side in an attempt to bring himself out of the dream like state he was currently in. He could hear her crying. He could feel her hand on his as she prayed that God would heal him and bring him back to her.

"Please come back to me," Naomi cried. She kissed the palm of his hand.

Naomi had been wrecked with grief as she watched him being pulled from the back of her car. She watched as they placed an unconscious Marquise on a stretcher to perform emergency surgery. Now, she sat patiently by his bedside waiting for him to open his eyes. She wanted to be the first face he laid eyes on and if that meant she had to wait forever, then so be it. She refused to leave his side for anything at all.

So many things were running through her head. What if she hadn't left him? Would he have been hurt if she'd never walked out on him? She blamed herself for leaving his side. Now that she knew she was carrying his child, there was nothing more important in the entire world then making things right between the two of them. All she wanted was to hear his voice again. To feel his touch on her skin and to see his smile. Marquise was hers and she refused to ever have to live without him.

Naomi's gaze shot up in his direction when she felt slight movement. She stood up and held his hand as she watched his eyes began to flutter. A wave of relief passed through her as she watched his eyes slowly open. Tears sprung to her eyes and a smile graced her lips as she was filled with nothing but pure joy. He'd come back to her.

"Baby, you're awake?"

Marquise continued to stare at her for a moment as his eyes adjusted to the bright lights within the room. Naomi kissed his hand and held it to the side of her face, allowing the tears to flow freely. She was in a state of euphoria. To see his hazel eyes once again was the most beautiful thing to her. There was no better feeling.

"I love you, Naomi," he cooed.

Naomi moved closer to him and gently kissed his lips before allowing her forehead to rest on his.

"I love you more, Marquise."

"You saved my life, bae. I probably would have died if you hadn't got there when you did."

"But you didn't. You're here with me right now with so much more living to do."

Naomi felt him shift slightly and his large hand rested on her stomach. She smiled while staring into his eyes. Honestly, she'd been so nervous about how he was going to feel about being a father, now that he was awake. She didn't mean to blurt it out the way she had, but she wanted him to know that he had a reason to fight. Their unborn child was that reason.

Naomi gently placed her hand on top his. She watched as a single tear fell from the corner of his eyes. Seeing him so emotional only made her cry more.

"I'm going to be a daddy?"

A happy chuckle echoed through her. A look of pure joy and excitement decorated his face.

"Yes, baby. You're going to be a father."

"How? I mean when did you find out?" he questioned with raised eyebrows.

"Well, I didn't know initially. But after I puked everywhere, I realized that I haven't had a period in a while. With everything that's been going on I didn't even pay attention. I don't know how far along I am yet, but I'm definitely pregnant," she admitted while nervously chewing on her bottom lip.

Naomi watched as the biggest smile she'd ever seen spread across his face. The way his eyes lit up erased any ounce of doubt she ever had. Marquise was happy and he was ready to take this journey with her. She knew that things wouldn't be a walk in the park, but as long as they had each other there was nothing that they couldn't get through together.

There was a brief knock at the door and they both turned to find the doctor entering the room. From the look on his face, Naomi could tell that he was pleased with the fact that Marquise was now awake. He approached him and began checking the machines while documenting and carefully observing Marquise.

"Welcome back, Mr. Lewis. Glad to see that you're finally awake," the doctor declared.

"Thanks, Doc, for everything," Marquise replied.

"Well, I can't take all the credit. Mrs. Evans here had a hand in that. If she hadn't got you here when she did you may have bled out."

Marquise turned to look at Naomi with loving eyes. She smiled while still holding his hand.

"The hard part isn't over though, sir. You'll need therapy to get that leg back in order. We removed the bullet from your leg during surgery and gave you a blood transfusion. It's going to take some time for you to fully heal, but in time you will."

Marquise nodded his head in understanding as the doctor continued to explain. Once he was sure Marquise fully understood the road he had ahead of him, he exited the room promising to come back in a few hours to exam his wound.

Marquise ran the tip of his fingers along the side of her face. He stared into her eyes, amazed at the woman he had standing in front of him. When he realized he was shot, none of the bullshit they'd been through mattered at all. The only thing he could think about was her smile. The way she said his name when he was buried deep inside of her. The way she loved him wholeheartedly. After speaking with his mother, Rose, she'd helped him realize just how fucked up his attitude had been towards her.

"Baby, I have something I need to say," he began.

Naomi sat down on the edge of his hospital bed with her fingers still intertwined within his.

"It killed me when you walked out the door and left me. I was sick as hell, Nao, and I didn't know what to do. You so damn stubborn and you didn't wanna hear shit I had to say. I felt like a piece of me died when you walked out of my life. I was so fuckin' mad at you," he confessed.

Naomi hung her head and swallowed the lump in her throat. She knew she'd hurt him bad. She saw the look in his eyes when she said those hurtful words. At the time, she felt her own heart shatter, too.

"Do you want to be with him, Nao? Do you really want to be with that fuck nigga?" he questioned with piercing eyes.

Naomi raised her head to look him directly in the eyes.

"No, Marquise! I'm sorry for what I said. I was hurt by your actions. You weren't spending any time at home with us and we'd barely been speaking. When we did talk, it's arguing and more arguing. Then the kids... Sometimes you seemed so irritated by them and it killed me."

"Nao, I know I haven't been the easiest nigga to deal with. I got a habit of holdin' shit in and then blowin' up when shit falls apart. I like to be in control all the time and sometimes I'm an asshole. But one thing about me is I'm loyal and when I love, I love with everything in me. All this shit is just new to me, bae, that's all, I swear. I can't be without you and the kids."

"I know, baby. We love you too, and I been so miserable without you. You were all I thought about and the more I tried not to, the more I cried. And when you called, I was on my way home to talk it out. When you told me you were shot... I thought I was never gonna see you again."

"Come here, baby," he demanded as he slid over slowly in his hospital bed. Naomi came closer, only for Marq to place his arm around her shoulder. Naomi lay next to him with her head resting on his chest. This was the feeling that she missed. The love... the devotion... All she wanted to do was get back to who they were before all the drama invaded their lives.

Marquise sighed as they lay next to each other in complete silence. The feeling of her in his arms was something he craved. He needed to feel her. He wanted her to be by his side, always.

"Where are my clothes?" he asked.

"What's left of them are in that bag in the corner," she confirmed.

"Bring it to me?"

"Right now?"

"Nah, later... yea' right now," he chuckled.

"Back to being bossy, I see," Naomi laughed, as she got up off of the bed and walked to chair in the corner of the room. She grabbed his bag that contained what was left of his belongings, and handed him the bag.

"I'm going to use the bathroom, okay? Be right back," she said before kissing him on the lips and stepping into the bathroom in the corner of the room.

Marquise quickly opened the bag and searched his pants pockets. They were obviously cut off of him, so he knew what he was looking for wouldn't be inside. He then searched through the rest of the bag and found his cell phone. He stuck his hand into one of his shoes and exhaled as he pulled out what he'd been looking for. Tucked neatly inside was a long, velvet box.

Marquise held the box in his hand before opening it to find a diamond necklace nestled inside just as he'd left it. He tossed the bag and the rest of his belongings on the floor beside the bed, just as Naomi came out of the bathroom.

"Find what you were lookin' for?" she asked as she shook the water from her hands.

"Yeah," he replied with serious eyes.

"You know if you wanted your phone that's all you had to say..." she spoke before her words trailed off.

Naomi hadn't noticed it before, but now that she'd come closer, she could see exactly what he was holding. She continued to walk towards him and then took a seat on the edge of the bed beside him.

Marquise stared into her eyes before brushing a long strand of hair from her eyes and tucking it behind her ear.

"Naomi... you're the best thing that ever happened to me. Before you, I didn't know where my life was headed. I was cold and in the streets more as the days went by. No woman on this earth has ever been able to have my heart like you do. You and the kids complete me. I want to wake up next to you every morning and go to bed next to you every night. I want be there for every baseball game and every recital. I want to be a family..."

Naomi smiled as he confessed his undying love for her.

"So do I. I want you to be there for everything. I know I was dead wrong and going back to Tyree was a big mistake. I thought what I was doing was what was best for the kids, I swear. I never wanted to be with him again, I swear. The thought of him touching me made my skin crawl. I love you so much, Marq, and I promise to always be by your side," she admitted.

Marquise opened the long box which held a diamond encrusted necklace. He'd purchased it as a gift for Naomi and planned on giving it to her before she'd decided to leave him for good. He'd been carrying it around ever since, so when the time was right he would be ready.

Naomi turned around to allow him to place it around her neck and fasten the clasp. She touched the necklace and could only smile from the thought that her man had put into her gift. Even after being shot, his main objective was to make her happy and he'd succeeded.

She quickly turned around and began planting kisses all over his face.

"Ah!" he yelled, causing Naomi to release him and look down at the leg she'd been pressing on with her elbow. She was so wrapped up in her man that she'd forgotten about his leg wound.

"Shit! Bae, I'm sorry."

Marquise winced through the pain, but continued to smile at her. He had his woman back and he couldn't be happier. He held her as she rested her head on his chest.

CHAPTER 23

"You love me?" he said as he planted sweet kissed on her lips.

"Yes, daddy! I love you so much!" she cooed as she held him tight.

"You still want to leave me?"

"No, never again, baby."

"You promise?"

"Yes, baby, I promise."

"I bet yo' ass don't, with how much I paid for them big ass rocks you got on," he teased.

Naomi playfully tapped his arm. She'd been touching the necklace ever since he'd put it on her neck. Marquise had given her gifts before, but to her, this one was special. It meant more. It was a symbol of everything they'd overcome.

Suddenly, two loud knocks sounded on his hospital door. Both Naomi and Marquise looked towards the door to see who was entering the room.

"Come in," Marquise yelled.

The door swung open and in came Rose. Naomi gave a friendly smile as she stood up to allow her to have access to her son. Although she wasn't sure if they had managed to make amends, at the end of the day, Rose was still his mother. Naomi felt in her heart that it was the right thing to do. If it were her in his shoes, her mother wouldn't have left her side. Because of that, she called Rose to let her know what happened to her son once he had awakened. Despite her shortcomings as a mother, she'd already lost one child. No mother should have to experience such pain in life.

"You must be Naomi," Rose said as she embraced her.

"Yes, I am. It's nice to finally meet you," Naomi politely returned the embrace.

"Thank you again for calling," she reiterated.

"You're welcome," she replied.

Marquise remained silent as he watched the two of them. He had no idea that Naomi had called Rose to let her know what happened. It made him wonder who else she called.

"Marquise, I'm so glad you're alright," she cried as she walked to him.

She stood at the side of his bed as if she were contemplating if hugging him would be a good idea or not. Naomi noticed her flirting with the idea as if she were afraid of being rejected. She glared at Marquise as she awaited his reaction as well.

"Thank you for comin'," he said as he extended his arms.

Rose leaned in and held her son tight before kissing his forehead. A wave of relief passed through Naomi. All she wanted to do was make things right and she prayed that she hadn't aggravated the situation between him and his mother by inviting her there.

Rose smiled weakly and took a seat in the chair next to his bed. She clasped his hand inside of hers.

"Well, what the doctor say?"

"I'm fine... I'll be out in no time."

"What he said was Marq will need therapy and it's going to take some time to heal," Naomi corrected him.

"Now that sounds about right."

"That's what I just said though."

Naomi rolled her eyes. "I'm going to step out in the hall to check on the kids. Will y'all be okay without me for a minute?"

"Yes, girl, go right ahead. I won't leave his side," Rose declared.

Naomi nervously chewed her bottom lip while contemplating leaving. She hadn't left his side since he arrived.

"Bae, it's okay. Get you some air and check on my kids," Marquise reassured her.

Naomi smiled before exiting the room and heading to the elevator. She decided to grab some snacks from the vending machine while giving her mother an update on his condition. She knew she would be worried sick if she didn't report something soon.

Marquise turned his attention to Rose who was staring at him lovingly. From the look in her eyes, you would never imagine that she would have done such fucked up things to him in the past. To Marquise, the hurt his mother caused no longer mattered. Now that he had been given a second chance, he was going to mend things with his mother and leave the past in the past.

"Your kids, huh?" Rose chuckled.

Marquise smiled as he thought about Christopher and Josie. All of the light they'd brought into his life made him a better person. They didn't know it yet, but they were a part of the reason that he'd become a better man. Because of them, he'd be ready for the new addition to the family when it was time. He no longer wore the doubts of parenting on his sleeve. He embraced and welcomed the idea with open arms. He was ready.

"Yeah, my kids. They not biologically mine, but nobody would know that if I didn't tell 'em," he clarified.

"Marquise, I am so proud of the man you've become. You did good for yourself... all without any help from me," Rose stated.

Marquise watched as tears sprung to her eyes.

"I told you all Naomi needed was some time. Didn't I tell you she'd come back to you?" she asked.

"Yeah, you did," he replied.

"Now that you have her back, don't get yourself hurt again! I'm here getting old and shit! My heart can't take it."

"I'll try... shit, tell that to the dead nigga that shot me."

Rose nodded her head in understanding. She didn't need him to tell her that he'd taken care of the situation. She knew exactly who and what her son was. Despite it all, she loved him with all her heart no matter what anyone had to say. To Rose, he was worth every ounce of pride she felt at the mere mention of his name. Marquise Lewis had grown into a successful, handsome, and amazing man. Dangerous as he was, she still loved him and understood he had to do what he had to do.

"I pray for you every night, you know. For our relationship and for my sins as a mother. I asked God to allow me to get a second chance at being the person that I wasn't strong enough to be all those years ago."

"I know you're sorry, Rose. I forgive you for everything and I want to move forward. But there's one thing you gotta promise me."

"Anything," she said as tears poured from her eyes.

Marquise hesitated before responding. "Promise me that you will be better for your future grandchild. Promise me that you won't walk out on him... Or her, like you did me. Be the woman you always wished you would have been to me."

Rose gasped as she clasped her hand over her chest. She smiled and rose to her feet to embrace him. She couldn't believe that she was going to be a grandmother. She couldn't believe that she had been given a second chance to redeem herself. This time she would do things right.

"Congratulations, son! I am so happy for you both!" she exclaimed.

Marquise just smiled at the warm response he'd received.

"You have an amazing woman, Marquise. That girl loves you so much! You're going to be a wonderful father."

"Thank you."

They continued to discuss everything regarding the pregnancy and everything surrounding his care after he was discharged from the hospital. Rose promised to be there to help them with whatever they needed. She ensured her son that all she wanted to do was make up for lost time. She promised to never let him down again. It was going to take some time for their relationship to mend, but Rose was prepared to do it all.

Naomi stepped back into the room just as Rose grabbed her purse preparing to leave the room.

"Are you leaving already, Rose? You can stay as long as you want," Naomi clarified.

"Oh no, hunny. I'm not leaving. Just going to grab a cup of coffee and get some air. This air is bothering my asthma, that's all," she assured her.

"Oh, okay."

Naomi went back to Marquise's bedside and climbed into the bed. She snuggled up next to him carefully, avoiding his leg. She nuzzled his neck allowing her head to rest on his chest.

"Bae?"

"Yeah?"

"Tyree put his hands on me today. When I tried to leave, he grabbed me by my hair and dragged me into his room."

Naomi dreaded telling him this at such a time. But, she knew she needed to be completely honest with Marquise. No more secrets no matter what.

Marquise's heart rate accelerated as anger resonated deep inside of him.

"Before you say anything, you're not in a position to do anything right now. I took care of everything. The kids won't be seeing him for a while and I already called my attorney after I whooped his ass good for trying me."

She looked up into his eyes to let him know she was dead serious about the ass whooping she'd laid on him. Although he was still angry, and she was positive he was still contemplating how he was going to kill Tyree, she knew he understood.

"I saw Erin today, too. I let her talk until she was got it all off of her chest and then I told her I never wanted to see her again. I'm changing my number in the morning."

"I'm proud of you, baby. You needed closure. Hey, who the kids with anyway?"

"They are with my parents and before you ask, yes, my mother knows what happened."

"And when she tells your father?"

"Who the hell cares? I'm still not speaking to him until he apologizes to you for being so rude and judgmental."

"Now aren't we being a hypocrite?" Marquise teased.

Naomi frowned and rolled her eyes. Even though she didn't want to hear it, she knew she couldn't stay mad at her father forever. She loved her dad, but his words cut her deep and she wasn't ready to forgive him just yet.

"I know, bae…"

Marquise kissed her forehead and began running his fingers through her hair. No matter how stubborn she was, he still loved her. He placed his other hand on her stomach once again. He rubbed in small circles as he prepared himself for what he was about to say.

"Baby, how do you feel about me legally adopting Josie and Christopher?"

Naomi turned her head so that she could look into his eyes.

"Where did that come from? I mean... When did you decide that you wanted to adopt them?" she queried.

"I been thinking about it for a while, lately. I was going to tell you the night you left. I wanted to show y'all just how much y'all mean to me."

Naomi smiled. "I would love that, baby. The kids would too. There are still some legal things that I have to sort through, but we'll take care of it together."

Marquise held her tighter. God, he loved this woman. She understood him and he appreciated her openness.

"I'm filing for a divorce, Marquise."

Marquise slightly sat up. Now he knew that Naomi was through with Tyree, but he also knew that she would never do anything that she believed would cause any emotional trauma to her children. When he suggested it before, she froze up. He needed to make sure that she was doing this because she wanted to and not because of anything he said.

"Are you sure?"

"I'm positive. We can't move forward with all the excess baggage dragging behind us. I want us to do this the right way and since you're adopting the kids, it's only right."

"I love you, Naomi," Marquise declared.

"I love you more, Marquise," she cooed.

They continued to lay in each other's arms. They now felt content, despite the curves that life had thrown them. At the end of the day, they had their health, they had their family, and most of all, they had each other.

***

"So this the pretty girl you been hiding from us, huh, Marq?" Kareem queried with a smirk.

Marquise nodded simply before grabbing hold of Naomi's hand.

"Yeah, man... this is her," he told Kareem and Sadie.

Suddenly, Anika and Blaze were walking hand in hand, and entered into Marquise's hospital room.

"B', you finally made it," Marquise greeted him with a smirk.

"Hell yeah I made it," Blaze said with a frown, leaving Anika's side so that he could move closer to Marquise's bedside. "You almost gave me a fuckin' heart attack, nigga. You a'ight tho'?"

"Yeah, I'm straight," Marquise responded simply. "If it weren't for my Queen right here comin' to my rescue when I called..." He turned to look up at the unknown female that had yet to be introduced to Blaze and Anika, with a sexy smile. "Lord knows I wouldn't have a leg no fuckin' more."

"That's where the bullet hit?" Kareem queried curiously, only to receive a head nod from Marquise.

"Wait, wait hold up... This is Nicol... I mean Naomi?" Blaze asked, looking from Marquise to the female right by his side.

Anika began to inspect her up and down, admiring her gorgeous facial features and how good she looked next to Marq. She was caramel, with long, straight, brown hair that went past her hips, and gorgeous, honey brown eyes.

Naomi did the same and began to inspect Anika. She was a beautiful, light-skinned chick with curly hair, big, brown eyes and a banging body. She looked so good alongside Blaze.

"Yup," Marquise replied. "This is Naomi y'all, my girlfriend."

Naomi shyly smiled at them and gave them all a little wave.

"Nah, fuck all that wavin' shit, don't be shy, bae," Marquise announced boldly, staring at her seriously as he reached for her hand. "This my family. You gotta be comfortable with them."

"I'm not shy, Marq," she voiced softly with a small smile. "Hey guys."

"Hey, nice to meet you," Anika greeted her warmly. "I'm Anika, Blaze's fiancée."

"It's good to finally know that Marquise's girlfriend ain't imaginary," Blaze declared amusingly, only to get a light hit from Anika on his chest. "Nice to finally meet you though ma, I'm Bl—"

"Blaze," Naomi said, cutting him off. "Marq's told me so much about you. And Kareem."

"Don't believe everythin' that nigga tells you 'bout us," Kareem informed her. "Especially the bad shit."

Naomi lightly chuckled before turning to Sadie. "And you must be Kareem's girl... Sadie, right?"

"The one and only," Sadie responded with a large grin. "I'm his fiancée, too."

"Bitch, what?!" Anika suddenly shrieked, running to Sadie frantically. "He proposed?"

Sadie quickly flashed Anika her left hand and they both started screaming and jumping happily at the diamond ring on her finger.

"Congrats, nigga," Blaze stated with a pleased facial expression. "Bout fuckin' time."

"Yeah, congrats, fool, but stop tryna steal the spotlight," Marquise joked. "I gotta tell you niggas 'bout the shootin'."

"A'ight, we listenin'," 'Reem responded.

Marquise explained how he was alone at the warehouse, and suddenly heard a loud banging of metal at the front door. He kept silent for a while, heard nothing, and decided to check the premises. It was then that he heard gunshots and when he finally got a chance to look at who was shooting, he saw Leek's face and aimed straight for the kill.

"One shot, one kill," Marquise stated. "One bullet to the head and he was finally down. I didn't realize I was shot until I started movin' again, so I knew I had to call for help. The only person I wanted next to me was Naomi, so I called her. I know I probably should have called y'all niggas, but y'all had just gotten back wit' yo' girls and shit, I didn't wan' to kill yo' moments yet. So Naomi came to get me, then I got here, they took the bullet out and now I'm straight."

"Well, you ain't exactly straight with that damn cast wrapped around yo' leg," Blaze pointed out.

"Yeah, but I'm alive and that's all that really matters," Marquise answered. "As for Jamal, y'all are just gon' have to find him without me and finish the plan."

Blaze and Kareem nodded at him firmly, knowing that for this to be truly finished, Jamal had to be sorted.

"Baby..."

Malik turned to his baby's gentle voice wanting to know what was up. He looked at her lovingly, waiting for her to continue to speak to him.

"Don't forget your promise," Anika reminded him seriously.

He nodded at her, trying to reassure her before speaking. "I promise I ain't gon' break it, sweetheart."

Epilogue

~ 6 Months Later ~

"Don't make me act up in front of all these people, Nao," Marquise firmly announced. "I want my kiss."

Naomi couldn't help but blush bright pink at Marquise's words. She was just awfully happy that they were back in a good place and things were so much better between them.

Naomi slowly leaned into his thick, juicy lips before giving him the kiss that he so desperately wanted.

They were currently at Blaze's Auntie Ari's barbeque, just enjoying themselves and taking in this happy moment they were living right now.

Auntie Ari's barbeque was in full swing, as everyone was either dancing, eating, or lining up to get some good, or either laughing and cracking jokes together.

"I love you, baby," Marquise whispered to her in between their deep kiss as he pulled her closer into him with his arms on her bare shoulders.

Only God knew how much he loved this woman and how he wanted to spend the rest of his life with her alone. He didn't want or need anybody else but her. He was extremely glad that they had worked out all their differences. Naomi and the kids had moved back in with him, too.

Things were going great and Naomi had already filed for divorce from Tyree, now she was just patiently waiting for things to fall through.

As for Marquise and his squad, things between The Knight Nation and Jamal Coleman had finally been dealt with.

Six months ago, Jamal Coleman had almost managed to kill his boy. If it wasn't for the fact that Jamal hadn't realized that he had an empty gun, then Marquise wasn't sure if he would have his best friend today, and confidently be able to say that he was going to stand as Blaze's best man for his wedding tomorrow. Alongside Kareem, of course.

Blaze and Anika's big day had finally arrived and tomorrow they were going to tie the knot as Mr. and Mrs. King. Marquise couldn't deny the fact that he was excited for the both of them. They were a part of his family and he wanted nothing but the best for them.

Speaking of family...

Things between Rose and Marquise were going well. They were still taking things slow, keeping things at phone calls only, and recently Marquise had been going to lunch with her. He knew that in a matter of time, things between them would be amazing. He definitely no longer blamed her for all she had done to him in the past. There was no point in holding on to so much pain and destruction. It was all in the past and Marquise knew for a fact that he needed to move on with his future.

His future with Naomi Lewis.

The more he continued to stare at her beautiful face, the more he continued to fall in love with her. And he knew for a fact that this woman sitting with him right now was his wifey for life.

***

Naomi sighed with happiness as Marquise drove them home. She was so tired after all the celebrations at Auntie Ari's barbeque, and she still needed to head back out for Anika's bachelorette party.

Naomi felt her eyes beginning to close as sleep began to overcome her, but the second she noticed Marquise pulling the car up, she was wide awake.

"Marq... Why are we here?"

She had noticed that he parked the car at an outdoor parking lot. And the more she began to examine her surroundings, the more she quickly realized where he had brought her. Their favorite beach spot.

"Close your eyes, Nao."

"Why?"

"Just do it for me," Marquise instructed, pecking her soft lips. "I know you don't really love surprises, but I promise you gon' love this one."

Naomi simply obeyed and before she knew it, she felt a silk blindfold placed upon her eyes. Then she was being led out of his car, then being carefully led to somewhere.

"Watch your step, bae," he whispered sweetly to her, holding her hand as he led her across the sandy beach.

Five minutes later, Naomi felt Marquise's hand leave hers and she was no longer being led to anywhere.

"Marq?"

The silk blindfold had been lifted from her eyes but she was quite nervous to open her eyes.

"Open your eyes, Naomi."

Naomi's eyes slowly fluttered open to see Marquise's hazel ones, and she watched on as he began to bend down in front of her and get on one knee.

Her heart began to race with joy and excitement and just seeing Marquise's nervous facial expression was bringing a smile to her face and tears to her eyes.

She began to examine their surroundings and she could see and hear the romantic scene Marquise had set up for her.

A choir of four female singers stood at a close distance to them and were singing the timeless classic "At Last" by Etta James. Red rose petals and white candles were neatly around them in a heart shape, and all Naomi could do was continue to smile with so much happiness.

"Baby, it's been a year since we first got together and I can honestly say that it's been a year well spent. You came into my life at such a dark time. I was rude, cruel, and out acting like a lil' hoe."

Naomi couldn't help but chuckle.

"But then you came along and changed me, Naomi. You changed me for the better and I thank God every day for bringing you into my life. I love you so much, Naomi Lewis, and I just want to marry you and seal the union we've already built together. It's just you and me, sweetheart, cause there ain't no other female on this planet that I want to spend the rest of my life with. You have my heart forever, no one else will have it. So I ask you this..."

Naomi's tears quickly began sliding down her cheeks as she watched Marquise lift a red box towards her and open it to reveal the gorgeous, breathtaking, and flawless diamond engagement ring.

"Will you marry me, Naomi Lewis?"

There was only one thing Naomi knew she wanted to say. This fine man right here was forever going to belong to her, no one else. Just thinking about it brought chills to her body.

"Of course I will, Mr. Marquise Lewis. I'm yours forever," she happily announced, letting him place the ring on her finger.

"And I'm yours forever, Mrs. Lewis," he concluded before getting up from his knee and pulling Naomi into his arms.

They began to passionately kiss, filled with so much happiness that they were going to get married. They had truly been through so much but through it all, they had come out stronger than ever. And Naomi knew that she was going to forever be...

Addicted to her thug.

~ The End ~

~ Thank From Ari & Miss Jen ~

Thank you so much for reading Ari & Miss Jenesequa's novel.

Please do not forget to drop a review on Amazon, it will be greatly appreciated and we would love to hear what you thought about this novel! Don't forget to check out Ari's other works:

- I'll Ride For My Thug 1 & 2 & 3
- Love, Betrayal & Dirty Money: A Hood Romance
- Young Love: Wrapped Up In A Thug
- Feel free to connect with Ari at:

https://www.facebook.com/Shakira(AuthoressAri)Brown

- And Miss Jenesequa's other works:
- Lustful Desires: Secrets, Sex & Lies
- Sex Ain't Better Than Love 1 & 2
- Luvin' Your Man: Tales Of A Side Chick
- Down For My Baller 1 & 2
- Bad For My Thug 1 & 2 & 3 {Blaze & Anika's Book}
- Love Me Some You
- The Thug & The Kingpin's Daughter

- Feel free to connect with Miss Jenesequa at:

https://www.facebook.com/AuthorMissJenesequa

www.missjenesequa.com

Please make sure to leave a review! We love reading them. Thank you so much for the support and love. We really do appreciate it.

Looking for a publishing home?

Royalty Publishing House, Where the Royals reside, is accepting submissions for writers in the urban fiction genre. If you're interested, submit the first 3-4 chapters with your synopsis to submissions@royaltypublishinghouse.com.

Check out our website for more information: www.royaltypublishinghouse.com.

Be sure to LIKE our Royalty Publishing House page on Facebook

CPSIA information can be obtained
at www.ICGtesting.com
Printed in the USA
LVHW021535060519
616793LV00001B/195/P